Second Chance with My Ex's Brother

A forbidden second chance romance

Ana Rhodes

Stardust Publishing LLC

Contents

PAIGE

"Paige? Paige, what happened?" Mia asked, running after me as I stormed into our apartment with tears streaming down my cheeks.

I tried to speak, but it came out garbled, even to my ears. Miraculously, Mia didn't need a translation. We'd been best friends since we were eight, and sometimes, I was sure we could read each other's minds.

"That lying son of a bitch! You were always too good for him," she hissed in response to my tear-laden explanation of my boyfriend of a few months unceremoniously dumping me. The man I was certain was "the one" had casually ended things. When I'd had the audacity to be upset, he'd turned nasty, telling me that if I hadn't been such a "cold fish," maybe he would've stayed interested.

Mia sat back. "Maybe Leo needs a reminder of what a cold fish really is. I say we start by shoving a bunch of supermarket fish in his tailpipe."

"Miaaaa ..." I drew out her name in warning.

"Oh! Oh, I know—stick a few beneath his mattress and turn up the heat," she suggested, her eyes lit up. "You still have his spare key, right?"

I bit back a laugh. Mia was stone-cold serious—and that was why I loved her.

"I saw that laugh," she said in mock outrage. "Laugh all you want, but I'll be adding a few pounds of scrod to my online order tonight," she promised before slipping away to the kitchen.

I listened as she rummaged around in the cabinets, then found one shred of calmness that allowed me to dry my face with the sodden tissue I didn't even remember plucking out of the tissue box.

How had I not seen it coming? Leo had been growing distant, but I'd chalked it up to his intense studying for finals. I still had a few semesters left before graduating from college, but it was Leo's last semester. He was about to take the LSATs, which would determine what law school he would attend. He came from a long line of lawyers: his grandfather, father, and older brother were all practicing. There was an expectation that everyone in the Townsend family would practice law, and Leo had been tearing his hair out for weeks preparing for the test.

I'd helped him with flashcards, timed practice tests, and scheduled study breaks with homemade meals to ensure his success. We'd even planned an end-of-the-semester party together in anticipation of his passing. It would be a big blowout for him and all his law school-bound buddies at his parents' lake house. Actually, Leo had secured the lake house while I hustled to plan the entire party because he was busy studying. Mia had warned me I was doing too much. "You have your own finals to study for," she'd reminded me.

To which I'd replied, "I know, but this is an important night for us—one we'll remember for the rest of our lives."

Soon after, when he'd met me after work to give me the good news he'd passed the LSAT with flying colors, I'd launched myself at him with a congratulatory hug. I didn't understand the uneasy look in his eyes when he'd set me down away from him and told me we were over.

"I mean, really, fuck that guy. After everything you've helped him with. Not to mention, you put all your plans on hold for him. You even changed career paths because of him," Mia fumed from the kitchen as I stared at the wall. Sadly, she was right.

I'd wanted to get a degree in business. Running my own business sounded like fun. I hadn't been sure what kind of business that would be until shortly before Leo and I had gotten involved. Recently, I'd started working at a fancy restaurant on the opposite side of town. Not only were the tips great, but I no longer left work smelling like a greasy spoon as I had at my previous serving job. The restaurant, *Bella Nova,* took its menu seriously. So much so, the waitstaff was required to take a wine education course so we could recommend proper pairings with the dishes. Since I'd only just turned twenty-one when I took the job, I knew nothing about wine. But in the last few months, I'd become intrigued and a little obsessed with the extensive process of creating an excellent wine.

When I'd mentioned my dream of opening a winery someday to Leo, he'd laughed. "You're telling me you're going to spend all your time learning about alcohol?"

"Well, yeah. It's a multi-million-dollar business if you can create a place for yourself. And I'm enjoying all the stuff I'm learning." I explained.

He'd smirked, and I should've read that as a red flag, especially as he added, "Sounds to me like you want to be a professional wino." I'd taken it as a joke instead of the insult it was.

Leo was smart and held himself with such confidence I never questioned him. Somewhere along the way, I'd lost myself and gotten swept up in the idea of being in a relationship and being loved.

I'd been so focused on being what I'd thought Leo wanted that I'd let him talk me into changing my major. He convinced me I should work at his law firm with him—not as a lawyer, of course, because he wouldn't want to compete against his girlfriend. But he'd said mediators were always needed. I hadn't completely understood what the job entailed, but when he'd described it to me, it sounded boring as hell. He'd sold it as something respectable and stable, so I'd agreed. I had been fighting my way through the classes, trying not to fall asleep—all for nothing.

"This sucks," I said from my place on the couch to Mia. "I mean, I met his whole family—well, most of his family. I've never met his older half brother. But I sent him a video message."

"You sent him a video message?" Mia asked, confused.

"Yeah, one time when I was at his parent's house, Leo's mom was worried because I guess his older brother was having a hard time. So, she went around recording everyone saying encouraging words to Wallace. But Leo couldn't be bothered, so she asked me to give him some encouraging words instead. I hadn't even met the guy, but she seemed happy with it."

"I bet his mom's going to be heartbroken over this one," Mia said.

"I know. I'm going to miss her. She was really nice. She made me feel like—like I was a part of the family."

Mia laughed. "I'm sure she wanted you to be part of the family ... I don't know any mom her age with a son who doesn't look at you and think daughter-in-law material."

I swallowed around the fresh lump of emotion growing in my throat. Yet another thing that sucked about the whole situation. Even though Leo and I had only been together for a few months, things had moved quickly. I'd already gotten to know his parents and was supposed to meet his half-brother Wallace at graduation. That wouldn't be happening now. I'd spent the last few months thinking I was marching toward my happily ever after, and he snatched it away just like that.

Mia returned from the kitchen with two steaming mugs of tea. I looked down at the murky liquid. "Don't worry, I put a little whiskey in there." She winked.

I smiled at her.

"It may not seem like it now, Paige, but you're better off without him. Somewhere out there is your knight in shining armor. I know it," she assured me.

"I wasn't looking for a knight in shining armor. I was hoping for a nice guy who would love me for me."

She nodded. "Well, Leo isn't that guy. But the right one is out there, and we're young, so there's no rush."

I nodded in agreement. "You're right as usual." I felt a little better after her pep talk when a text message alert on my phone chimed. I lunged for it, thinking it might be Leo, and I was right. But the words that met my eyes were not flowery words of regret and professed love. Instead, they read:

Hey, I know what went down between us is still a little raw, but would you mind getting a hold of the DJ for the party and asking him to be here an hour earlier?

I let out an angry sigh.

"Oh, no, what does it say?"

I handed Mia the phone and watched her eyes nearly pop out of her head as she read the text. "The nerve of that asshole. I mean, he stomped on your heart, and now he's worried about this stupid party."

"Yep. A party I drove myself to distraction over planning. Nitpicking every single detail instead of studying more for my finals," I fumed.

Mia looked at me for a moment, and then a wicked grin spread across her mouth. "The party you and I are going to crash," she said.

I sat up from the couch. "Oh, no, how humiliating would that be?"

"Not at all, and I'll tell you why. You're going to put on your sexiest dress and strut into that party like you own the place. He's going to realize how bad he fucked up while you and I have a grand old time dancing with cute guys."

I shook my head, recoiling at her suggestion.

"Come on, Paige," she pleaded. "I understand you're hurt, I do, but do you want to shrink away that easily? This guy needs to understand he can't behave that way. If he wanted to end the relationship, fine, but he could've had some compassion."

"You won't get any argument for me," I agreed.

"Think about it, Paige. Think about all the things you've changed and sacrificed for this guy. It's time to take it back."

As I plopped down on the couch, a fresh wave of mortification rolled over me as I thought about all the changes I made to be a "better fit" for him. I'd changed my major, career path, and a hundred other little things to make him happy. Somewhere in all that, I lost myself. I never used to twist myself into a pretzel to make somebody happy, but I'd become a complete doormat in my quest for love and companionship.

I'd watched my mother cater to my father's every whim. It was in those rare moments when we were alone I experienced how vivacious and fiery she was. I remember being flabbergasted she wasn't naturally a mousy, subservient woman. But after so many years with my father, she'd folded herself into what she thought was a much more palatable version of herself—at least for him.

It made me resent him and his bullishness, and I wondered why she stayed with him. By the time I'd left for college, I'd accepted that people stayed in relationships for their own reasons, and it was between them. She was an adult, and as much as it broke my heart to watch her hide her sassy side, I knew I had to continue to be the force of nature she raised me to be. For both of us. Then I met Leo ...

It wasn't like he'd asked me to change everything about myself. I just followed the example I was shown my whole life.

"Wait a minute, what's going on here?" Mia said, waving her hand in front of my face. I pulled myself out of my contemplation and looked at her with determination.

"I had a major epiphany," I said, feeling stronger that I had in a long time.

"Oh? Tell me," Mia said with raised eyebrows.

I took a deep breath before admitting, "I think I was just mimicking my parent's relationship. Without realizing it, I was following in my mother's footsteps."

Mia looked at me, then added, "I believe that's what Oprah would call a lightbulb moment."

I laughed. "Something like that, but I think you're right. I planned the damn party. Why shouldn't I enjoy it?"

Mia clapped her hands together. "All right! That's my girl! Now, we need to go shopping for some new outfits. Operation: 'Make the Boys Sweat' is underway," she said in a singsong voice as she floated to her bedroom.

I had a smile on my face even as uncertainty settled at the bottom of my stomach. If I was going to stop being the doormat I'd become over the last few months, I would have to make some big changes, no matter how uncomfortable they were. I already had a long list in my head of everything I needed to do to reclaim my life. But first, I needed to show up at that party and show Leo exactly what he was giving up.

"I don't think this is such a good idea anymore," I whined as we neared the lake house.

Mia looked at me sharply. "I love you, but if you say that one more time, I'll have to give you a sisterly slap."

"You'd really do that?"

"If it's what it takes to snap you out of this, then yes. It's all out of love, of course," she said.

I rolled my eyes and shook my head. "I'm getting more anxious the closer we get to the lake house. This will be the first time I've seen him since he dumped me, and I feel like such a loser."

"But you're not a loser. Don't get in your head about this. Come on, you're dressed to the nines, and you look sex-eee," she said, drawing out the last word. "And I look pretty good, too," she said.

I laughed. "We both look pretty good," I admitted.

"We're stunning, but what's going to make us go from looking good to knockout is how we walk into that party. So, tell me again," she insisted, wanting me to go over the plan for the hundredth time. It was getting annoying, but I couldn't blame her, considering my nervousness.

I sucked in a long breath, then recited, "We go in head held high, hips swaying, and we talk to everyone but Leo."

"Exactly!" she said with a decisive head nod. "And, if you can find yourself a stud muffin and start chatting him up, that would be icing on the cake."

I laughed. "I don't know. I know most of Leo's friends. Some are cute, but I'm not sure any of them qualify as a stud muffin ... Where did that term come from, anyway? Your grandmother?"

"Hey, Granny has some pearls of wisdom, so what if her terms are a little outdated?" she countered.

I relaxed and focused on Mia's words as we approached the lake house.

I'd been there before with Leo's parents, and it was beautiful. It was empty most of the time, and I knew his parents were thinking about turning it into a vacation rental for tourists. I'd had fun decorating the place for the party. Several times in the last three weeks since I'd been in and out of the house setting up, I stopped to watch the sunset over the lake.

Although the house was a little big for my taste, the view was stunning. When I looked out of the big plate-glass window in the living room toward the backyard, I spied a pier that stretched over the lake's edge and led to a guesthouse. I hadn't seen the inside, but it looked like the perfect place to escape for a little while.

I knew if I got overwhelmed during the party, I could look out the window and escape to the guesthouse on the water. I'd even revealed my plan to Mia, who'd replied, "Don't you be escaping to that guest-house. You need to stay present and hot—that's our mission."

When I'd looked a little terrified at the thought, she'd reminded me, "My phone is on me—the second you need to go, just text me, and we'll get the hell out of there."

I remembered that promise now and took comfort in it. I was so lucky to have her as my best friend. There was no way I'd survive without her.

I rubbed my sweaty palms over my thighs, tugging at the short hem of my dress. It was a sexy little sundress that hit mid-thigh, with spaghetti straps over a peasant bodice with a little keyhole tie at the front, revealing an ample amount of cleavage. It was the most risqué dress I'd ever owned, and I felt self-conscious. When I'd slipped it on in the store, Mia had assured me it was the dress that would make Leo eat his heart out. I paired it with some strappy sandals and swept my hair back into a French roll with loose curls framing my face. I felt overdressed for a casual lake house party—but we were going for sexy, and Mia assured me it was.

Every time I shifted in the car seat, I felt my boobs slip farther out of my dress, and it was a little nerve-racking to know I was revealing so much. When Leo and I were together, I'd dressed more conservatively. The memory irritated me and made me stick out my chest a little more.

It was time to get the old Paige back, and she never would have given a shit about how revealing the outfit was.

As Mia found a place to park, I took a deep breath before exiting the car. She rushed around the front to grab my hand. "Remember who you are. You are Paige-fucking-Russell, a woman not to be messed with," she whispered in my ear as we walked into the party.

The place was already bustling, and the drinks were flowing. I noticed Leo had added a keg, which I'd argued against, but I knew there would be a couple of bottles of wine in his parents' wine cabinet. I would find my way over there at some point. In the meantime, I braced myself against the onslaught of rowdy partiers.

"Dammit, I should not have had that big ass soda before we got here," Mia said, squirming next to me.

"There's a bathroom down the hall to the left," I said, pointing toward the restroom.

She looked at me with uncertainty. "I do not want to leave you here alone."

I patted her on the shoulder. "I'm a big girl. Paige-fucking-Russell, remember? I'll be okay. Find me when you're done."

She gave me a grateful look as she leaned in to say, "Nine o'clock. One of those stud muffins is checking you out. You can thank me later," she winked before rushing to the bathroom.

My gaze went in the direction she'd pointed and met a pair of intense, dark eyes watching me.

I felt the blush crawl down my body along with the man's eyes. He was tall, broad-shouldered, and shameless in how he looked at me.

I swallowed around the nervous lump in my throat. I've never had a man look at me like that before. He was unfamiliar—and older than everybody else there. I wondered who he was as I turned to walk away.

I wandered through the house, greeting people I recognized and congratulating those still sober enough to understand what I was saying.

As I slowly made my way to the wine cabinet off the side of the kitchen, I heard a playful giggling and a familiar voice.

I stopped in my tracks, following the sounds. It was coming from Leo's father's office. The door was ajar, and when I looked inside, I glimpsed an ass I recognized all too well—Leo's.

My eyes traveled upward, and I saw his ass drilling into a beautiful girl I recognized from one of his study groups. Her head was thrown back, and her hands clutched his shoulders as he fucked her over the desk.

Everything inside me went cold. Did they even realize the door was open, or did they just not care?

I sucked in a breath and got my feet to move, rushing away from the scene of the crime. Except it wasn't a crime, was it? Leo and I had broken up. What he did was none of my business anymore.

I made it to the wine cabinet and selected my vintage of choice with a decisive flourish. I poured myself a generous glass, took a large sip, and tried to erase the image replaying in my mind.

Leo had always wanted me to do something wild like that, but I didn't want to disrespect his parents' home, especially if I would be a part of the family.

We'd had plenty of sex, but we could never be too boisterous. There was always a roommate on the other side of the wall or his family down the hall.

He was always grooming me to be a lady—to conduct myself as a future lawyer's wife. I had to be put together at all times. I guess now I understood what he'd meant when he'd called me a "cold fish." He wanted someone to bend over his father's desk. I didn't hate the idea, though now I hated the idea of it with him.

I looked up from behind the kitchen island, and once again, my mystery man's eyes were on me. He was much closer now though still a respectable distance away. He was close enough I could tell they were dark brown ... and they were looking at me like I was naked.

Emboldened by heartbreak and anger, I held his gaze as I brought my wineglass to my mouth and took a healthy swallow. One side of his mouth quirked up, bringing my attention to his full lips. He had some stubble on his face, and I wondered what his stubble would feel like against my skin.

"Paige," a whisper came next to me, and I nearly jumped out of my skin. Mia was next to me now. She teased, "I see you and stud muffin have progressed to eye fucking. I have to say I'm proud of you."

I rolled my eyes. "We're not eye fucking. I just happened to look up, and he happens to be very nice to look at. Besides, it's a pleasurable distraction to forget what I just saw."

Mia looked instantly intrigued. "Spill."

I rubbed an agitated hand over my face. Dropping my voice to barely above a whisper, "I passed by Leo's dad's office, and he was in there, screwing some girl over the desk."

Her eyes bugged out of her head. "You have got to be shitting me? Did he see you? Did you say something?"

"No, and no, what would I say? 'Oh, hey, sorry to interrupt. I'm crashing your party, but please continue fucking this bimbo."

"I'm sorry, Paige. That's rough."

I nodded in agreement, feeling a fresh wave of disgust. "I'm not sure this was a good idea. I want to go home," I told her.

Mia set her lips in a grim line. "Paige Elizabeth Russell," she said, "I do not want to be insensitive to your situation, but you need to rally, girl. Your ex of two seconds is in there, screwing some other girl. Meanwhile, you've got tall, dark, and brooding over there, undressing you with his eyes. Why don't you go over and talk to him?"

"I wouldn't even know what to say to him. Not after what I just saw," I huffed.

"Look, if you really want to go, I'll take us home. I'm just worried that once we get there, you'll feel worse, and I am sick of Leo making you feel bad. He's ruining your fun. So, forgive me for being pushy, but I don't want that asshole to dictate yet another decision for you."

I glared at Mia because she knew those words would trigger me. I didn't want to be controlled by any man despite the last several months of girlfriend servitude with Leo.

"Okay. I get your point," I told her. "Have you thought about becoming a motivational speaker or a life coach someday?"

Mia's eyes brightened. "You know, that's not a bad idea." She reached up and twisted some of my stray curls. "Stand straight, chest out, and go get him. Just text or scream out the safe word if you need a rescue."

"We have a safe word?"

"Duh. Just holler 'MUFFINS,' and I'll be there in a jiffy!"

I laughed, "Okay, granny."

She looked at me. "I mean it. If he ends up being a creep, these heels double as a crotch stabber," she vowed.

"Got it. Wish me luck," I said, scooping up my glass of wine as I worked my way toward the mystery man.

The place was getting more crowded by the second, and I lost track of Mr. Tall, Dark, and Brooding. The disappointment I felt surprised me as I did a slow three-sixty around the room.

I was about to admit defeat when I felt a tap on my shoulder. I spun around, sure it was Mia. Instead, I was looking up into deep, soulful brown eyes and a sexy smile. "Excuse me, were you looking for me?"

"Yes," I breathed before I could stop myself. "I mean, no. I noticed you earlier from across the room, but ... I was looking for my friends," I lie.

"Oh, that's a shame. I was hoping you were looking for me," he said, stepping closer, overwhelming my senses with a sweet, musky scent.

"You were?"

"I was. I saw you walk in here with your friends and then rush off to the kitchen," he said, his eyes looking over my face.

I bit my lip. "Oh, yeah. I went to get a glass of wine."

"There's still wine left? I would've expected Leo to have plundered it all by now."

I laughed. "No, I tried to get him into wine, but he never developed a taste for it. Which, I guess, is why he got the keg."

"Yeah, well, Leo isn't known for his refined taste," the man said.

I looked at him with a slightly furrowed brow. "How long have you known him? Have we met before?" I asked. I didn't remember meeting the man, but he seemed to know Leo well.

He shook his head. "No, I would've remembered meeting you," he said in a silky voice, and then he stuck out a large hand. "I'm Miles. It's good to meet you."

My racing heart kicked up another notch as I slowly reached out my hand to shake his. His fingers enveloped mine, and warmth shot up my arm. He squeezed my hand and didn't let go.

"Paige," I told him.

"It's nice to meet you, Paige," he said with a smile. "Tell me, are you one of the graduates?"

I shook my head. "No, I still have a couple of semesters to go."

"And let me guess—then you're going into the oh-so-exciting field of law like the rest of these sheep."

I laughed at his mock horrified expression. "No, I mean, I was for like a second. But I think I'll be changing my major back to business."

"Business? Good for you. What kind of business are you going to get into?"

I hesitated for a moment before answering, but as the words came out of my mouth, I realized they were the truth. "Wine. I'm thinking of starting a winery."

His eyebrows shot up. "That's interesting, not something you hear every day."

"Yeah, I know. Not everyone understands, but I love learning about how to harvest grapes and make wine. It's an interesting fusion of science and art, and it's fascinating."

He looked at me for a moment with an odd smile framing his lips, and I tensed, waiting for him to offer some smart-ass comment. Instead, he dipped his head lower so he was closer to me and said in a conspiratorial voice, "You know, Sonoma is a perfect place for what you're talking about. They already have quite a few wineries, but it's one of the most beautiful places on earth. Especially when you see it from the sky."

"The sky?"

His smile grew. "Yeah, I started accumulating hours to get my pilot's license a while back, but life got in the way. During one of my practice runs, I flew into this little airport in Sonoma, and it's gorgeous."

I smiled at him. "I'll take your word for it. Are you going to finish getting your license?"

He looked at me as if the idea had just occurred to him. "I think I will. There was a time when I thought it was behind me, but I've missed it so much lately. It's important to focus on the things that spark joy even when everything else feels out of control."

The hairs on my nape stood up.

I laughed. "I always say that. I wish more people understood it."

He nodded. "It's a hard lesson to learn. I'm trying to do better myself, though."

"Me, too," I whispered, looking at those bottomless, brown eyes. A girl could get lost in those eyes, and there was something about that five o'clock shadow on his jaw that made me want to reach out and touch it. Instead, my fingers fiddled with the stem of my wineglass.

"So, tell me about your ideas for the winery," he said, leaning in so we could hear each other better.

It was getting louder at the party, and all I wanted was to listen to Miles's deep, sexy voice.

Looking around, I asked, "Do you want to go someplace quieter so we can hear each other better?"

He gave me an easy smile. "I've got the perfect place."

MILES

*S*everal hours prior ...

All I wanted was some peace and quiet. To be away from everybody.

But life seemed to have other plans.

Ever since graduating from law school and joining my father's firm, it had been a constant grind. All I did was work ... There were no vacations and rarely a weekend off. And as the runt at the law firm, I got a lot of crap got dumped on me. But I understood the hierarchy of the place and probably wouldn't mind it if I didn't hate being a lawyer.

I still remember having a panic attack before taking my LSATs, calling my father, and telling him it wasn't for me. He'd laughed and said it was just nerves. Every Townsend man was a lawyer, so I would be a lawyer. Case closed.

I hadn't wanted to disappoint my father, and what I'd really wanted to do had seemed so eccentric compared to what everybody else in my family did. I'd tried to sell my father on the idea that I could fly commercially and make good money doing it—but he'd laughed in my face, disinterested in my lack of passion for the law.

"Wallace," he'd said, using my first name—no matter how often I told him I preferred to be called by my middle name. "Your flying business is a nice side hobby; that's what you reward yourself with after you win a case. But you need a proper job for an actual adult. You're not Peter Pan."

Easy for him to say. He loved his job.

After only a few years into being a lawyer, I'd already been to the emergency room with an ulcer, and I was absolutely miserable. It'd all come to a head a few weeks prior. After an intense slog with a case, I'd finally called my father and told him I needed to take some time off. He'd laughed at that, too. Lawyers didn't take time off.

But I'd told him it was necessary. My body was breaking down, and my mental health was in the tank. My spirit was lost. I'd hung up on him before he could argue with me.

Not long after, my stepmother, Lucy, had called. God love her. She tried so hard to look after me, but my father was a force to be reckoned with. When my mom was still alive, my stepmother was aloof. I'd gotten the sense she'd been worried about stepping on my mother's toes. But since my mom had passed, Lucy had taken her role as my de facto mother seriously.

She'd called me to say I'd done the right thing, "If your body is telling you it's time for a break, then that's what you should do."

"Even though Dad says it's some 'sissy shit'?"

"Oh, you know your father. He loves his job more than anything. I don't think he gets it when others don't feel as passionately about the same things he does. I'll talk to him. But in the meantime, you do whatever is necessary to take care of yourself."

I'd promised her I would. A few days later, she'd sent a video of various family members giving me motivational messages. Even my father had begrudgingly said, "Get better, kid. We need you back at the firm."

My stepmother had filmed her friends cheering me on, telling me to be easy on myself. She'd filmed my little brother, Leo, although he'd been distracted, glancing between my stepmother and his phone, saying, "Yeah, feel better or whatever."

In the background, somebody had exhaled and reprimanded him gently, "Leo, I think he needs a little more than that."

The next thing I'd heard was my stepmother saying, "Paige, why don't you say something?"

The camera had swung to an olive-skinned girl with wide green eyes and long, wavy sable hair. She'd looked uncertain. "No, no, I couldn't. We've never met."

My stepmother had responded, "He can use all the encouragement we can muster. It doesn't matter who it's from."

After sucking in a deep breath, the beautiful young woman had said, "Hi, Wallace, I'm Paige—nice to meet you ... sort of. I'm sorry you're going through a difficult time, but just remember to hold on to the things that spark joy even when everything else feels tough. Hold on tight, and they'll pull you through any hard time."

"That's very wise, Paige," my stepmother had commented. "Now you listen to her, Wallace. Those are words to live by."

I'd watched that video a few times and the part with Paige more than a few times. Something about her pulled at me. I couldn't quite put my finger on it. Aside from the fact she was gorgeous, she had a sparkle in her eyes that was half playful and half passionate, but she'd looked like she was desperately trying to keep it in check. Then there was my idiot brother sitting beside her, completely unaware of the gorgeous, passionate woman sitting next to him with a sweet smile and even sweeter words for a perfect stranger.

I'd told myself at first it was the stress of the last few years that had me feeling so unhappy with my life, and I was desperate for any spark of light—that had to be why I was so drawn to a thirty-second clip of a woman I'd never met.

But I would soon find out it wasn't just my vulnerable state that drew me to her.

My few days off turned into a few weeks. My father was upset, but I couldn't return to the firm. I was thirty-one years old, long past allowing my father to call the shots, yet that was what I'd allowed him to do for years.

I'd desperately needed a change of scenery, and my parents' lake house seemed like the perfect fit. I'd remembered it being a peaceful place as a kid. Because I was the oldest, I would often stay in the guesthouse to have some privacy from everyone and the hyperactive Leo.

We used to go a few times a year, but it had hardly been used since Leo had grown up and I moved out ages ago.

My plan had been to hole up in the guesthouse for a while and take in a few of those amazing sunsets over the water. It may not have helped me figure out my life, but it would definitely have made me feel better.

Plus, it had given me an excuse to get some flight hours in. I sneaked a few here and there since I'd started practicing law, but it had been a long time.

After a few trial runs with an instructor to regain my bearings, I'd felt confident enough to fly out to the lake house. Being back in the air was incredible, and I'd instantly felt like myself again. I'd landed on a private airstrip close to the lake house that belonged to a neighbor.

I didn't know what my future held, but I knew I had to fly more because it had been a balm for my soul.

The lake house had been quiet as I'd set up in the guesthouse. I'd only been there a few hours before I saw Leo's car pull up. I met him in the drive, curious why he was there.

That was when I found out he was throwing a big ass party—some celebration for finals and passing the LSAT.

"Mom and Dad didn't say anything about you throwing a party," I said.

He laughed. "That's because Mom and Dad don't know. They would throw a hissy fit if they knew I was throwing a party at their precious lake house. But it's not like I'm going to mess it up, and I'll clean everything afterward. You're not going to rat me out, are you?" he asked.

"Why do you even need to have a big party? Can't you take your girlfriend somewhere nice and have a celebratory dinner or something?" I asked.

He made a face and said, "She and I broke up."

I wanted to ask questions, but that would have been too obvious. Plus, it would also mean I'd have to examine the bloom of hope in my chest at his announcement. I hoped she was okay.

"I'm sorry to hear that. Are you okay?"

He'd shrugged like it was nothing. "I'm the one who broke it off. I didn't want to be tied down. Paige is the marrying kind, and I'm interested in the freaky kind right now if you know what I mean," he'd said with a conspiratorial grin.

I grimaced.

"How long is this party supposed to go on?" I'd come here for peace and quiet, not to be subjected to a college frat house party.

"A few hours. It's a small get-together of friends—nothing big or raucous," he assured me.

"You promise?"

"I promise. You won't even know we're here."

"Fine, they won't hear anything from me," I said with a sigh. "Just keep it down, okay?"

"You got a big bro."

I headed back to the guesthouse, wondered if Leo's ex-girlfriend would come to the party, and then instantly felt guilty. I could only imagine what my brother would think if he knew I watched Paige's video every night before bed. My intentions were totally innocent. Her sweet voice was the only thing that could soothe me enough to sleep.

A few hours later, the pulse of the DJ's music shook the pier and guesthouse. I was sitting on the edge, dipping my toes in the water, trying to ignore the rowdy noises, but it was becoming too much. If I had to hear one more person screaming "Duuuude" only to be answered with another "Duuuude," then I was liable to lose my shit.

I tried to tune out all the noise and focus on my breathing so I could plot out the flight path for the next adventure I wanted to go on with my rented Cessna 172.

But I was interrupted by what sounded like a cat coughing up a hairball; only, we didn't have cats. I looked over, and several yards away, a young woman was bent over the edge of the water, puking up her guts. Her friend's obnoxious voice pierced the air. "I told you you were a lightweight, Shannon. No more wine coolers for you. Here, drink some beer to wash down the barf."

"Jesus Christ," I muttered. That was when I decided enough was enough. I walked toward the main house, slipping into the side door. I was on the warpath to find Leo and give him a piece of my mind ... when I saw her.

Paige.

She stood in the foyer with another young woman, looking uncertain.

While I was surprised to see her there, something else washed over me that was unexpected and hard to identify. Was it relief? Excitement? Maybe a little of both.

She caught me staring, but for the life of me, I couldn't look away. The woman who'd been my savior for the last several weeks was now a few yards away from me in the flesh.

My eyes followed her as she moved toward the kitchen, and when she disappeared from view, I felt a pang of regret.

Maybe things had ended more amicably between Leo and Paige than I'd thought. But when I watched her gulp down her wine, I suspected that wasn't the case.

If I had to guess, my brother was up to no good, and Paige was having to pay the price. That was when her eyes caught mine, and she started walking toward me. My heart started pounding. I hadn't felt that kind of rush since I was a teenager.

Once we started talking, I completely forgot she was Leo's ex-girl-friend. She was just a beautiful woman, and I was more relaxed than I'd felt in a long time. The way her face lit up when she talked about opening a winery was intoxicating. My stepmother had mentioned something about Leo's girlfriend possibly going into the firm with us. I suppose a lot of things were changing for Paige after the breakup.

I thought about telling her I was Leo's older brother, but I quickly squashed that idea. She was clearly there to take her mind off things and have fun. I didn't want to ruin it for her. She was full of passion as she talked about her plans and asked a lot of questions about my flying, which I was all too happy to answer.

I couldn't help but inch closer to her. She smelled so damn good, and when she bit her lip like she was uncertain about something, the blood rushed to my cock.

I needed to tread lightly here. She and Leo may have broken up, and my brother and I haven't always gotten along, but I wasn't one to lust after someone else's girl.

Except she wasn't someone else's girl anymore …

When she asked for someplace quieter, I knew I was in trouble. The lake house was packed, so as I led her through the crowded room, I instinctively reached back and grabbed her hand. The feel of her hand in mine again was dangerous. It felt so small, so soft, and so ... right. When I glanced over my shoulder at her, the heat in her eyes reflected the heat I also felt.

That was when I stopped trying to justify my watching her video repeatedly. It wasn't simply because she was calming. Something else drew me to her, and as I pulled her out into the fresh night air, I knew I was in deep shit.

I led her to the pier and walked to the end, just a few feet from the guesthouse.

We sat down at the end of the pier, and I watched avidly as she took off her shoes to dip her toes into the water. "I hope you don't mind," she said.

"No, I don't mind at all," I said, my eyes never leaving her face. My gaze drifted down to her lips, which parted as she watched me. "Is this quiet enough for you?" I asked.

A slow smile took hold of her beautiful lips, and she bit the bottom one—I wanted so badly to lean across and bite it for her. She tipped her face toward the stars. "It's so beautiful out here."

"Yes, it is," I said, keeping my eyes on her.

She looked at me then, and I caught her eyes trailing to my mouth. "You're very easy to talk to," she said.

"I'm guessing you're not used to that," I answered.

She shook her head. "Not so much—not with guys anyway ... Well, not with the last guy I was with."

"I'm sorry to hear that. He missed out."

"Oh, I don't know about that," she said, and when I protested, she put her hand up. "I don't mean to sound like I'm feeling sorry for myself. I'm not. I—I'm realizing we weren't well-suited for one another. We wanted very different things."

"And what do you want?"

She sighed, looking back across the water. "I want peace, I want adventure, something I can be excited about."

"All good things. What else do you want, Paige?" I asked, needing to know more.

She let out a sigh and gave me a coy smile. "I want you to kiss me."

My mouth dried at the request. Paige laughed nervously. "That was really forward. I'm sorry, I shouldn't have ..."

I leaned forward and pressed my mouth to hers. My hand cupped her jaw, and any guilt I felt evaporated.

She was so soft and yielding I couldn't help but take her mouth possessively. Those sweet lips melted beneath mine. I slipped my tongue inside, groaning when hers met mine. She met me stroke for stroke, and I went deeper, feeling like I would never get enough.

She let out a soft moan as my hand skated across her waist, around her back, and pulled her closer to me. Her softness against my hardness made something claw inside me—need, want, desperation—urging me to get her as close as possible.

The voice of reason in my head shouted at me to slow down and remember who she was. It was bad enough I was mauling my little brother's ex-girlfriend, but what was worse was she didn't know she was making out with her ex-boyfriend's older brother.

Alas, I'd been having a hell of a time listening to my voice of reason lately. The voice that told me I should suck it up and go back to the job that was making me hate my life and fly as a hobby. Now, it was telling me not to kiss the hell out of the beautiful woman who'd asked me to—and that was when I decided to hell with the voice of reason.

My decision was almost instantly rewarded as Paige's hands grasped at my shirt and yanked me closer. My last shred of logic and control was gone. I wanted the woman. I needed her.

I almost cried aloud when she pushed me away, gulping in air, her eyes wide.

"Look, I just got out of a terrible relationship, and I'm not in any state to be starting something new with someone else," she said, watching my reaction carefully.

"Okay, I understand that," I said, even as part of me broke inside. I didn't know what I expected her to say—I just knew my heart was still pounding, and my cock was as hard as a rock.

"I'm tired of always doing the right thing ... doing what others expect of me. I want to do something for myself for once," she said, placing her hand on my chest.

I waited with bated breath as she licked her lips. "One night," she said.

"One night?"

"One night, no strings attached. We just have fun and then go our separate ways." I looked at her, slightly stunned for a moment. "You and I both sound like we need a fresh start. Why not start with a bang, so to speak?" she said with a small, hopeful smile.

I didn't answer her. Instead, I stood up and looked down at her, hoping the ferocity I felt clambering inside me wasn't showing so obviously on my face. I didn't want to scare her away.

Then I went down and hooked my hands beneath her armpits, brought her up, and slung her over on my shoulder in a fireman's carry. She squealed as I turned on my heel and marched a few feet to the guesthouse door. "I'm guessing this is a yes?"

"You better believe it. This is a fuck yes, Paige," I said as I swung her off my shoulder and back onto her feet. She swayed, laughing, as

I pulled her to me, kissing the smile from her lips and pressing her to me.

I kicked the door shut behind us without letting go of her mouth.

I was tired of thinking about repercussions and futures and expectations. At that moment, a beautiful woman had offered herself to me, and I would be a fucking idiot if I didn't take her offer and run with it. So I pushed the thought of my brother and what it might do to him out of my head. He was an idiot for letting her go. And I would make her feel appreciated and worshipped. I would right the wrong he'd committed.

So I set about making sure she didn't have a shred of doubt about her choice. I kissed her until she could barely breathe, gasping for air as she clung to me.

I'd spent so much of my life the last couple of years feeling restless and untethered. But Paige made me feel high and yet anchored to something solid.

She pulled back from me abruptly, breathing hard. "Now it's your turn to tell me what you want, Miles," she said seductively.

I huffed a small laugh. "I'm not used to being asked that."

"Well, I'm asking you now."

I didn't want to scare her away, but she and I had an unspoken truce to be completely honest with each other, so I told her exactly what I wanted from her.

PAIGE

"I want to lay you on that bed and taste every inch of you," he told me as he stepped forward and gently cupped my face. He continued, "I want to know what your sweet little pussy tastes like. I want to eat you until you're shaking beneath me and screaming so loud you make that noisy party next door sound like a library."

I felt my mouth fall open, and he took advantage, leaning down and nipping playfully at my bottom lip.

"And once I'm done tasting you, I want to push my cock so far inside you that you won't know where you end and I begin. And then I want to fuck you until neither one of us can think straight."

I felt my mouth go dry. I'd never been so wet in my life. How could I not be ready for Miles and his dirty mouth?

At a loss for what to say, I stepped back, and he looked dismayed at having to release me. But when he saw my hands go for the hem of my dress, I got a flash of those dark eyes dilating and his breath quickening. I threw the dress off to the side and stood before him in my lacy bra and skimpy panties, feeling empowered as I watched the way his hands clenched into fists by his side.

I bit my lip, holding back a smile, and took a step toward him, reaching for his shirt. But Miles was in no mood for a slow striptease because he grabbed me and carried me to the bed, laying me out across it.

He peeled off his t-shirt and then shoved his pants down his legs, leaving him in boxer briefs with a very prominent erection for me.

Then my eyes met his, and he asked, "Do you like what you see?"

I nodded as I propped myself up on my elbows. He didn't move for a long moment—just admired me. I grew impatient, desperately needing to feel his touch. I sat up and hooked my fingers beneath the waistband of his boxer briefs, yanking them down.

He was beautiful. And big. All I wanted to do was get my hands—and mouth—on him.

His husky chuckle called my attention back to his handsome face. "There will be plenty of time for that later. First things first—I need to know what you taste like," he said, leaning over me and gently pushing me back onto the bed among the pillows. Then, his mouth was everywhere. I couldn't keep up with the sensations racing along my skin as his mouth sucked at the delicate flesh of my neck and his hands explored my body.

He reached behind my back with one hand and effortlessly unhooked my bra, dragging it down my arms and tossing it aside.

I gasped when his hands gently grasped my breast, his thumb flicking over the hard nipple as his tongue tasted my skin. When his mouth finally closed over my nipple and sucked it gently, my back arched off the bed uncontrollably. I needed to get closer to all the delicious things his mouth was doing to me as he went back and forth between my needy breasts. His hands wandered down my sides and over my hips, dragging my panties down with them.

Then his hand slid up my leg, his fingers dipping into my wetness. I couldn't stop the moan that escaped my lips. I moved my hips, silently urging him to continue.

He lifted his dark head from against my skin, looking up at me from his position with a hard nipple at his lips. "Somebody's anxious," he teased.

"Yes, somebody is," I said with a quiet warning. Heat flared in his eyes, and he held eye contact as he dipped his middle finger inside my pussy, working it in and out. That alone was enough to have me rolling my hips against his hand, but when he moved his thumb to work over my swollen clit, I let out a full-out cry.

There was something about how Miles worked my body, watching me intently, that had me feeling hotter than I'd ever felt before. Never in my wildest fantasies had I been this worked up, and I felt like a different person with him.

Maybe it was the build-up of all the misery I'd experienced until this point. Maybe it was being at the guesthouse, knowing my ex was a few hundred feet away. Or maybe it was a combination of all those things that made me so hypersensitive, but I needed Miles inside me.

"You know what you said about tasting every inch of me?" I asked.

He smiled and nodded. "Along with all the other things I *will* do."

I nodded. "Yeah, I'm in for all of that, but can it wait until after ..." I trailed off.

He looked at me with a mischievous glint in his eyes, and I knew he wouldn't let me off the hook. "After what, Paige? Tell me," he demanded.

"After you fuck me," I said. "I need to feel you inside me. Now."

His eyes darkened, and he got off me and left the bed. He returned with a string of foil packets. He ripped one open and made quick work of rolling a condom onto his hard shaft. Then he was poised between my thighs.

I thought his hands felt good between my legs, but when his hardness teased my opening, I knew I was in for some serious pleasure.

He leaned over me, looking serious. "You want me inside you, Paige?" I nodded. "How badly do you want it?" he asked, nudging his tip at my entrance.

"I have never wanted anything more in my entire life. Please ..." I pleaded.

And with that, he pushed into me, his impressive girth stretching me wide. He went slowly at first, but I urged him on. "Miles, more, please, more."

Something inside him snapped, and then he was drilling into me, mumbling through gritted teeth, "If my girl wants more, I will give her more—especially if it's my cock. That's it. Squeeze that sweet little pussy around me."

I cried out in pleasure, and I cried out for more. Miles was right. I didn't know where I ended or where he began, and I didn't want to. I kept crying out for more, and he was happy to oblige as he whispered filthy things in my ear about how good I felt and everything else he was going to do to me that night.

Listening to every dirty word that came out of his mouth pushed me over the edge faster than I expected. "Miles, I'm coming. I can't stop," I told him breathlessly, and I saw a satisfied spark appear in his eyes.

"That's it, Paige. Come for me. Show me how much you love my cock." His words coiled through me like a thread, with each syllable tightening the thread until the spasms grew too strong, and I clenched around his hardness like a vice. I screamed out my orgasm, and he went faster, his release following shortly behind me. "That was so good, my sweet girl," he cooed into my ear as he collapsed on top of me.

We laid there, listening to the thunderous riots of our heartbeats as we caught our breath.

After a few long moments, Miles pulled back and said, "That was amazing," as he kissed me long and slow. That kiss turned into a long make-out session that felt more sensual than any of my other previous sexual encounters combined.

I was breathless once again by the time he moved down my body and proceeded to taste every inch of me as promised.

I lost count of how many times I came that night—and got lost in those dark eyes that could see right through me.

For a moment, I let myself entertain the notion we could carry on beyond the night, but something in me shut down the idea—it was time to face the world on my own and live on my terms. And that meant saying no to the beautiful, dark-eyed Miles.

I clung to that thought as I slipped from his bed as the first rays of the sun shone through the window. Miles and I had fallen into a satisfied sleep some time ago, but I had a feeling from how he was whispering in my ear before we fell asleep he might give me a battle when we woke up, so I needed to make a clean break as we'd agreed the night before.

Not long after my second, or maybe it was the third orgasm of the night, I'd told Miles I needed to use the restroom and text my friend so she wouldn't send out a search party for me. I'd told Mia I'd taken up with the dark-eyed stranger for the night and gave her my location, just in case. She'd told me she was going to head home, but she'd be back in a flash if I needed her.

Now I was taking a very satisfying walk of shame home, away from Miles, the guesthouse, and Leo's parents' lake house, heading toward a nearby gas station where I would meet the ride share I'd ordered.

The entire ride home, I was conflicted. I wanted desperately to turn around and go back to Miles, but there was also a lightness in my chest I hadn't known for a long time.

Things would be changing soon, and for once, it was because I was taking charge, not because someone else dictated them. I was terrified but also more excited than I'd ever been in my entire life.

I'd taken a massive chance by spending the night with a handsome stranger, and it had paid off in spades. Now, I hoped to take that luck into my next venture.

MILES

Going to sleep with Paige in my arms, I felt a peace I hadn't known for a very long time. I didn't know what the morning would bring us, but I thought we needed to have a frank conversation about our "one night" agreement. I wasn't one to go back on my word, but if there was ever a moment where I should, it was then.

I fell asleep inhaling her scent and feeling completely relaxed for the first time in ages.

Waking up the next morning with her gone ... just gone, no note, no sign she'd even been there, was misery.

Her leaving with no way for me to reach her made it clear she meant what she'd said about keeping it a one time thing. The last thing I wanted to do was push her away.

I sat on the edge of the bed, rubbing my head and trying to figure out what move to make next. When I finally stood up and started getting dressed, I halted when the smell of her wafted from the sheets. That simple reminder made it click for me—I decided.

No more waffling. No more feeling bad. And no more trying not to disappoint everyone around me. Paige had told me the night before she was taking her life back, and if she was brave enough to do it, then I needed to be brave enough to do it, too.

For a few brief hours, I tasted, held, and touched the beguiling combination of peace, excitement, and enjoyment.

I might never get to hold Paige again, but at least I got to hold her for a night, and now I felt strong enough to chase joy, peace, and excitement in my everyday life.

With that thought, I dressed and walked with determined steps to the lake house.

Trash littered the floor, and I had to step over a few random people who were passed out as I made my way to my brother's room. I didn't bother knocking. I busted open the door, and it swung back, hitting the wall behind it. He looked at me with squinted eyes and growled. "Dude, why do you have to be so loud?" His voice didn't even stir the young woman who was laid out across him, still dead to the world.

I felt my lip curl. That was what he decided he wanted instead of Paige.

I shook my head. I supposed I should have felt worse for having done what I did with my little brother's ex-girlfriend the previous night, but I didn't, not one bit.

"You need to get these people out of here and clean this place up in the next hour, or I'm calling Mom and Dad," I announced. I was tired of covering for his ass, and he needed to learn the consequences of his actions.

"Bro, what the fuck? I thought you were cool," he whined, but I didn't care. I was tired of trying to keep everybody happy. What was it doing for me? It left me with an ulcer and anxiety.

I turned around to leave the room, and my gaze fell on a picture wedged behind the frame in Leo's mirror.

It was a picture of the beautiful girl who'd been in my arms a few hours before.

I glanced behind me to see Leo sitting up in bed, rubbing his hand over his face and not paying one bit of attention to me. I marched to the door, shot my hand out, and grabbed the picture from the mirror before shoving it into my pocket.

Maybe I was inviting heartache, being able to look at her beautiful face whenever I wanted to, but having a picture of her made me feel stronger. Paige had become my inspiration for taking my life back.

One night with her would never be enough, but it was enough to make me snap out of my daze and go after what I wanted.

PAIGE

Eight years later...

"Well, it looks like you've had another successful tour, my fearless queen of wine." Julian bowed.

"Yeah. Did you notice the guy who came over to me after the tour was over?"

"No, was he cute?" Julian asked, waggling his eyebrows.

I sighed. "He asked if he could propose to his girlfriend in the vineyard. Do you know what this means?"

He made a pouty face. "Another guy off the market for you."

I rolled my eyes. "Why is it always about men with you? This is good news. They propose in the vineyard, take millions of pictures, post them on social media, and tag Ambrose Vineyards. It's free publicity."

"True, but I take offense to your question. I have an active love life, so sue me."

"I thought things were going well with Danny?" I asked, referring to Julian's latest main squeeze.

He waved a dismissive hand at me. "Of course, they are, but I like to keep my options open."

I made a face, mostly because Danny was so nice.

"Hey," he said defensively. "At least I give myself options, little Miss Sleeps-by-Herself."

"Okay, judgy. I don't have time for options. I have a winery to run. And we're opening this resort soon—there's too much to do."

"Yes, sweetheart, but I want you to have someone to make you happy," he argued.

I huffed. "I don't need another person to make me happy, especially not a man."

"Is this the part where you tell me you're into women now?"

I shrugged. "No. I'm not into anybody right now—male or female."

"And that's why I worry about you. At the very least, you should be getting some on the regular."

I laughed and rolled my eyes. Ever since we'd become friends, Julian had been extra concerned about my lack of a sex life. It just wasn't something I focused on. I'd gone on plenty of blind dates, and I'd even had a few long-term partners. But after those disasters, I resigned myself to the fact I'd already had the most amazing sex I would ever have, and I was doubtful it could be replicated. In the moments when I longed to go back to that guesthouse with Miles, I reminded myself that that night had not been wonderful just because of the sex but because of the beautiful, kind man I'd shared it with. That night had been the turning point I'd needed. It was because of that night I was standing in my very own winery at that very moment.

After my night with Miles, I kicked my life into high gear, adjusting priorities to my needs and wants. It was like I'd completely rid myself of my protective shell.

I put myself out on the line to go after everything important to me. I'd changed my major and doubled down on my schedule at school so I would graduate on time. Mia and I had taken monthly, sometimes biweekly, trips to wine country. She wasn't as into the science of wine-making as I was, but she was into consuming it, so she was a happy and willing partner in adventure.

I spent all my days and nights learning everything I could about vineyard management and winemaking.

That was another part of my life touched by Miles. He'd been the one to recommend Sonoma, and as soon as Mia and I had traveled there, I'd instantly felt at home. That feeling only grew when I met a nice older couple who ran a small winery in town. I would make return trips with and without Mia and talk for hours with the couple about how they'd started and made the place grow. I'd shared my dream of starting my own winery one day and told them I was determined and excited about the future.

By the time I'd graduated from college, I was so friendly with the couple they came to my graduation. And then they gave me the opportunity of a lifetime. "Come work at our winery, Paige. We want to show you the ropes," Mrs. Ambrose had told me.

I had been so grateful for the opportunity, but as Mr. Ambrose continued, I'd been left in a state of shock. "Mrs. Ambrose and I aren't getting any younger, and we'd like to retire someday, but we don't want to see all our hard work go to waste. We want to make sure it's in the hands of somebody who loves it as much as we do." That was when he'd taken both my hands in his and said, "Paige, we believe that's you. We never had children—the winery was our baby. Come work for us, learn everything you can, and when you feel ready, take over Ambrose Winery."

Fate had smiled on me. I'd put out into the universe what I wanted, and it had answered. All those years later, I still felt like I was walking on cloud nine, but that didn't mean I didn't work my ass off.

It would be a few more years before I would be in complete control of the winery. After the first three years, the Ambrose's had told me they thought I was ready, but the idea of doing it alone panicked me, so I'd convinced them to stay for a little longer.

As time wore on, I gained more confidence, but I was relieved when I met Julian.

Julian was a regular at Ambrose Winery and a good friend of the Ambrose's. He recognized that taking on the decades-old winery at twenty-five might be a little cumbersome. So, he offered to join me as a partner. I would focus on the vineyard and winemaking while he would continue doing what he loved: traveling the world and discussing wine and other cultures with anybody who would listen. Except now he would discuss Ambrose Wines exclusively. Julian had a magnetic personality and could talk to anybody. Within sixty seconds of talking to someone, he would turn the conversation to Ambrose Winery, which made him the perfect spokesperson for our little business. Plus, over the years, he and I had grown close. Next to Mia, he was my best friend.

While I'd met more than a few of his boyfriends over the years, he'd never seen me with a man, and he voiced his concern regularly.

My lack of a love life didn't bother me. The winery was the great love of my life, though that didn't mean I didn't spend some nights, okay, most nights, thinking about what could've been.

I'd accepted Miles and I were only meant to spend one glorious night together, but we had to go our separate ways to live our dreams. And I couldn't complain about how my life turned out.

But it didn't stop me from wondering what had happened to him. I thought about him more than I did any of my exes. It wasn't like I knew his last name, so I wouldn't have even known where to look for him.

Every time I got a little too fixated on my memories of Miles, I reminded myself I was living my dream and I needed to focus. And the focus had paid off. Once the Ambrose's had retired and Julian and I had taken over, we increased revenue and exposure in leaps and bounds. In three years, Ambrose Vineyards had blown up. It was now a driving force for getting tourists and elitists alike to find their way to sleepy little Sonoma. It had become a destination for many proposals, and we'd hosted several weddings.

Those weddings started the seed of an idea that we were now in the throes of executing.

In a couple of months, Ambrose Vineyards would not just be making wine, giving tours, and offering wine-tasting classes; it would also be the home of Ambrose Vineyards Resort, a small and exclusive resort that catered to a unique clientele looking for a once-in-a-lifetime experience.

We broke ground a year ago and, piece by piece, put the resort together amid many setbacks because of everything from weather to permits. But soon, we would open the doors, and I was so excited—and terrified. The resort wasn't something I'd originally envisioned, so I'd be lying if I said it didn't keep me up at night worrying whether I could handle it.

Maybe that was why I'd thought about Miles so much lately. My night with him taught me that some of the biggest risks had the greatest rewards. I'd taken a chance with him, and it'd ended beautifully.

So, I took some chances in business. They were calculated and well thought out, but they were risks, nonetheless. Luckily, I had a business partner willing to take those risks with me—sometimes more so—which created some friction. But lately, we'd agreed on most everything, and it had calmed my nerves to know I wasn't alone.

Julian's eyes suddenly lit up. "I almost forgot to tell you! I have some fantastic news," he said, rubbing his hands together in glee. "You know that delicious pilot who takes me back and forth," he said, referring to the charter plane he used to get to and from Sonoma. Julian came from old money and had a trust fund that allowed him to go where he liked whenever he liked. That wasn't to say he wasn't a good businessperson and a hard worker, but he played exceptionally hard. He claimed Sonoma was much too small for him as his home base, so he lived in Los Angeles. He flew in using a charter plane service at least once a week to go over the plans or check in with me. He and the pilot had struck up quite the friendship.

"Let me guess, you got his number?" I asked as I went through the ledger to look at the numbers for the day.

"No, unfortunately, he doesn't swing that way—believe you me, I found that out the first day I flew with him. But he's just a doll. In fact, you and he would be pretty cute together." I shot him a sharp look, and he hastened to continue. "Well, the dishy pilot's little brother just got engaged, and they want to throw an engagement party."

"Fantastic. When can I start setting up the venue?"

"Next week. I know that's a bit of a time crunch, but I think this could be fantastic publicity for the resort."

I looked at him, confused. "The resort? Or the vineyard? Because we still have a few months before the resort opens."

Julian grimaced and then tried to cover it with a bright smile. I knew that smile. He was up to something. "I was just thinking ... now, hear me out before you completely freak."

"Too late," I muttered.

"I was thinking it would be nice to do a trial run, a soft open, as it were."

"We already planned a soft open for two months from now, Julian, not in a few days."

"I know, but I got caught up in the excitement of things, and my pilot has been so accommodating. He was talking about how this was a big moment for him and his family because they've been estranged, and he wants to help his little brother celebrate his engagement. I just wanted to help him bring all that together... I enjoy bringing people together. You know that," he said, blinking rapidly at me.

My hands clenched into fists by my side. "That's all well and good, Julian, but you're asking for entirely too much. There are still several rooms that need to be painted. Not to mention, we have to make sure the water is working and decorate. I mean, for God's sake, there's still scaffolding out by the pool. We're going to look so unprofessional and unprepared."

Julian was shaking his head. "Don't you worry about that, darling. These are nice people. If his family is anything like he is, they'll be perfectly understanding."

"We don't want them to be understanding, we want them to be impressed. We want them to tell their friends this is the place to go," I fumed.

Julian had the good grace to at least look a little sheepish. "Okay, I made a bit of a boo-boo. Listen, it's going to be a tall order, but I think we can pull it off. Besides, they're getting their stay for free, which means they'll be more willing to overlook the unfinished touches."

I glared at him, and he withered beneath my gaze. "How about I get you an iced coffee? Your favorite—with extra whipped cream?"

"This cannot be fixed with an iced coffee, Julian," I said, panic setting in.

"Sorry," he said, looking apologetic.

I sighed. There was no use in getting upset. I didn't have time to be upset. I just had to get the place together in time.

"I'm sorry to put us in this position, Paige. It felt like a good idea at the time."

"It's all right. I knew when we partnered up, you were a bit ... impulsive."

He sniffed. "I prefer spontaneous."

As I gave him a disapproving look, he backpedaled, "But I can see where you would say impulsive. So, what are we doing now?"

"First, we make the mother of all lists, and then we call in every favor owed to us because we're going to need an army to make this happen."

Julian snapped his heels together and saluted me. "Aye, aye, captain! I'll start calling in the troops."

I watched Julian saunter off from the small landing that overlooked several rows of vines sprouting clusters of deep purple-hued grapes. As he disappeared from view, my attention shifted to the field, and I sucked in a deep, cleansing breath. Whatever obstacles we faced, there was nowhere else in the world I'd rather be.

"Right, then, time to get on with it," I said. Then I marched to my office and began putting together the extensive list of things that needed to be done over the next few days.

By the next morning, I had every friend and employee waiting in the winery's tasting room.

"I really appreciate everyone being here to help us out. Please know I will be forever in your debt, and if you need anything from me, I will do whatever I can to help."

I looked out at the small crowd of people. I would have to pay my employees overtime, but it was worth it. Besides the staff, Mia had driven up from the San Francisco to help me out. I could always count on her to help whenever I was in a bind.

"I ordered an assortment of breakfast foods. There are muffins, breakfast burritos, pancakes, and waffles. So, everybody, fuel up, and then let's get to work," I said, clapping my hands together. Everybody dispersed to get their food, and I ran over to Mia, wrapping my arms around her in a big hug.

"I'm so glad you're here," I said to her.

"You know I'll always be here whenever you need me," she yawned. She worked late the night before, sleeping maybe three hours, and then drove to Sonoma.

"You wouldn't be so tired if you'd just move here," I told her again.

Mia had been working in public relations in San Francisco since we'd graduated from college. She was great at it and had more than enough work, but she was envious of my laid-back Sonoma lifestyle. I'd been trying to convince her to move here for the last couple of years. She worried there wouldn't be enough for her to do, but when we expand the winery, we'd need somebody with her skill. And if the resort did well, it would bankroll her position, so a lot was riding on its success.

"Don't start on that again. When this town needs a high-powered public relations genius, then I will be here in two seconds flat. In the meantime, I'm still paying off my student loans, so it will be a while before I retire to a small town."

"Who said anything about retiring? I'll put you to work. Maybe not in PR right off the bat, but I hear you have some skills with a paintbrush," I teased.

"Oh, God, is that what I'm doing today?"

"Correction: You and I are painting rooms," I told her with a bright smile.

Her shoulders slumped.

"Hey, I figured it was better than spackling, and I know you don't like anything to do with dirt, so I kept you off the landscaping crew."

"I thought I would do a little light decorating, maybe oversee the others," she said, pushing back her hair.

"We'll get there. But first: Paint," I told her.

She shook her head. "No, no, no, first, it's breakfast burritos—you better have chorizo and eggs," she said, wandering off to the breakfast bar.

I followed behind her and loaded up my plate. We spent the next half-hour eating breakfast and going over our plans for the next few days. I reviewed the list with everyone, and we divided tasks, agreeing to meet at the end of each day to review what we'd accomplished.

The next few days would be long and tedious. The employees who wanted to stay for overtime did, thank God. But the others drifted in and out as they could. Mia had to return after a couple of days, leaving Julian and me to finish up.

"Julian, I'm worried. We only have a few days before the guests arrive, and we still don't have plumbing complete in the back half of the resort."

"You worry too much. We'll keep the guests in the front half of the resort. Besides, we only need—let's see," he said, counting to himself. "Two, three, four, no, wait, six—six rooms total. We can handle that."

"Six? Since when? I thought it was only a few people. How big is this pilot's family, anyway?"

"Well," Julian started, looking a little red. "There's the pilot, his parents, his brother, and the fiancée," he listed off.

"Okay, but that's only three ..."

"And then an associate of Danny's—he's very richie-rich and loves checking out start-ups. And then, the travel blogger I mentioned ..."

I shook my head. "No, no! You told me it was just the pilot and his family," I hissed.

Julian's eyes widened. "I didn't? I could've sworn I had."

"What's this about a travel blogger? That is the last thing we need right now with nothing ready to go. It's one thing to pretend we're ready for one family, but now you have a travel blogger who'll write up a review and eviscerate us for our lack of preparedness. What were you thinking?"

"I was thinking we always pull through and make it work," he said before adding, "I believe in us."

"Are you kidding me?"

"What? You don't believe in us, too?"

"Well, of course, I do. But I also believe in more practical things like gravity, that there are only twenty-four hours in a day, and we only have two days left before these people get here. Now, we have to bulk up the menu, order more food, and make sure more rooms are ready. How in the hell—"Julian cut me off by placing his hand gently over my mouth. I looked at him in warning.

"Shhh, just shush," he said encouragingly. "It's going to be okay, Paige. You need to breathe."

"If you don't take your hand off my mouth, I'll bite you," I mumbled behind his palm.

He snatched his hand away and gave me a tight smile. "Look, I wanted to tell you about the others, but you were so stressed out, and I know we're going to get it all done, so it would be okay. And I was right. The place looks magnificent."

Julian went on about all the wonderful things that would happen because of the visit. And once again, the differences in our outlooks were obvious because while he was waxing euphoric about how it was the start of a beautiful new endeavor for us, my mind was racing with everything that needed to be done.

I stormed out of the room midway through Julian's litany of all the wonder that was about to happen. I couldn't handle it at that moment, and I spent the next half-hour pacing, trying to calm myself down even though I had no time to waste.

When that didn't work, I marched out to the vineyard and inhaled the taste and smell of the grapes. That was my happy place. I needed to get a hold of myself before I marched back into the building.

I closed my eyes and focused on my breathing. Then I wandered to my other happy place—the place I didn't allow myself to visit very often because while it made me happy, it was also bittersweet.

I found myself back on that pier, looking into the dark, soulful eyes of the most handsome man I'd ever met. He was so encouraging and told me I could do anything I put my mind to.

I would visit him occasionally so he could give me a pep talk when everything was too overwhelming and I wasn't sure I could pull it off.

Having renewed my strength, I sucked in a deep breath, set my shoulders back, and headed back into the building. Time to get to work.

MILES

"One more pass, " I told myself as I turned another loop around the sleepy little town of Sonoma. Although, it had hardly been sleepy lately.

When I'd first started flying commercially, it was not the hot spot it was now. I frequently flew people back and forth from LA for wine tours and classes. One of my faithful passengers, Julian, who was part owner of a vineyard, was constantly filling my ears with stories of his winery and how wonderful it was. I also heard all about how wonderful his business partner was. He never mentioned her by name, but I'd gotten the sense he was trying to set us up.

That was why I'd avoided his invitation to the vineyard until now. I wasn't interested in a setup. Years ago, I'd spent one unforgettable night with the most beautiful woman I'd ever laid eyes on. No one I'd met since has ever compared. I still longed for Paige, though it would have been wise to let go of the memory and move on. But the night we'd spent together did more than leave me wanting more of her. It had cemented my courage to take charge of my life.

After I'd left my parents' lake house, I'd put in my resignation at the law firm and turned off my cell phone. I knew my father would call me incessantly to talk me out of it and remind me of my "responsibilities."

I was all too aware of what my responsibilities were, and they weren't to him. I had to live life on my terms, and I was done living my life for other people.

With a decent nest egg set aside from my years as an attorney, I'd taken some time to accumulate flight hours and get my pilot's license. Once I'd had enough hours, I'd caught on at a charter company. I'd known a lot of powerful people from my time at the firm, so I'd used the same address book to secure clients. Through word of mouth and a solid reputation, I was flying high rollers and celebrities in no time.

I'd be lying if I said I didn't get lonely from time to time. While I loved all my adventures, if I could go back in time, I would have snatched Paige up and taken her with me. I thought about her often, but I vowed never to look for her. She'd left without a word that night and made her intentions clear. I didn't want to pressure her by chasing after her.

There was a self-help guru I used to fly back and forth to conventions a few years back who'd insisted that if you loved something and it was meant to be, it would come back to you. It was an old adage, and even though I'd never bought into that self-help mumbo-jumbo, something about what she'd said resonated with me. Or perhaps I just really wanted to believe she would come back to me.

After several years of flying, I'd started to feel restless—like it was time to make another change.

I'd been making more trips to Sonoma, particularly because of Julian. And I would stop to fuel up or just look around. There was something about the place that felt like home, and even though it was a tourist destination now, it was still a fairly small, slow-paced town. After all the hustle and bustle of flying all over the world, slowing down was looking like an attractive option. Lately, I'd toyed with the idea of purchasing my own airplane and getting a hangar at the local airport. I liked the people I worked for, but my end goal was to have my own business.

That longing for a slower pace and a soft place to land had hit me harder when I found out my little brother was engaged. He'd been dating the woman for a while, and they seemed well-suited. I'd only met her a few times. She didn't hold a candle to Paige, of course, but she seemed sweet, and she grounded my brother in a way I'd never expected.

He'd done a lot of growing up in the last several years, and he was genuinely in love with the woman from what I'd heard from my stepmother.

Sadly, Leo and I had rarely spoken over the last few years. Christmas was tense, with my father still being pissed at me for leaving the firm, and any other gathering mostly consisted of my poor stepmother trying to make conversation and get everybody to talk to one another.

So, when Julian asked me if I wanted to visit the vineyard, my knee-jerk reaction was to tell him no. But then he started telling me about the resort he and his business partner were adding to the vineyard, and they needed to do a soft opening to get some feedback. He offered to have my family and me enjoy a free week at the resort. I'd initially told him no, but when I was flying home later that day, I thought about how it might be the perfect opportunity for my family to heal the rift that had grown over the years. A week together welcoming a new family member sounded like a good idea.

I would never defend what Leo did to Paige or how he behaved throughout college, but he'd grown up and was starting a family of his own. Then there was the news my stepmother let slip during one of our weekly phone calls about my dad's latest diagnosis. Now, more than ever, I felt the urge to get my family together.

Of course, I'd have to avoid whoever Julian was trying to set me up with. It wasn't like I hadn't dated in the years since Paige, but no one had ever come close to making me feel the way she did.

Sometimes, I was certain I'd already had the great love of my life. And other times, I laughed it off, telling myself I was overthinking it, making it a bigger deal than it was.

When I called my parents to suggest the idea, my father was reticent, but my stepmother was excited enough for everybody. It would give me a chance to speak with my dad and little brother and celebrate Leo's engagement. If nothing else, it was a free trip.

My stepmother was convinced it would be a great way for my father to get to know his soon-to-be daughter-in-law. He'd never gotten to know, much less remembered the name of, any of the women Leo and I had dated.

Finally, everyone agreed. We would fly to Sonoma for a week, and I couldn't shake the feeling another enormous shift was on the horizon.

The day we were supposed to fly into Sonoma, everything had gone wrong in every way imaginable. Our flight was delayed because of some inclement weather near Los Angeles, and then my brother was called away because of an issue with some case he'd been working on. His fiancée stayed behind with him, and my stepmother had elected to as well. I smelled a setup because it would force my father and me to have more "quality time" on the flight.

Making conversation with my dad was no easy feat. If he wasn't talking about a case, he had little interest in much else. I even had him sit in the cockpit—figuring he'd be more comfortable with me instead of in the back with the other guests. I also thought it would be an opportunity for him to experience what I did for a living.

But as we took off, things began on a sour note as my father asked, "Are you sure you know what you're doing with this thing?"

I gave him a tight smile and replied, "Of course, I do. I've been doing this for a long time now, Dad."

"Seems like a perfectly good waste of talent to me," he muttered to himself, and I pretended I didn't hear him. I really didn't want to fight with him.

After pointing to various sites and getting noncommittal answers from my father, I offered, "Do you want to steer the plane?"

He looked at me like I had grown two heads, but I rushed to assure him, "It'll be fine. You won't crash the plane or anything. You have a skilled pilot watching you." I smiled proudly.

"I leave that to the professionals. I mean, isn't that what you are now, son?"

A familiar wash of anger swept over me, but I held it in check. If it were a normal situation, I would've let him have it, but knowing what I knew now about his health, I bit my tongue and laughed off his question. "Of course. Eight years under my belt, thousands of flights. I would say I'm a professional," I said.

"Good," he said shortly. "If that's what you want to call it," he muttered again under his breath.

Despite my best efforts, I had to accept he would probably never approve of my career as a pilot. Instead of getting riled up, I went to my happy place in my head—and wondered what Paige was doing.

I'd managed not to look her up all these years because I figured it would be much too painful if I found her, and she wanted nothing to do with me. But I worried now I would be in one place for a week with so little to occupy my time that I might give in and try to find her.

"Are we supposed to be dipping this low? Or are you just showing off?" My dad's terse question pulled me away from my thoughts about Paige.

"Yes, Dad, we are supposed to be dipping this low. We're coming up on the airstrip, preparing for landing."

Out of the corner of my eye, I saw my dad fussing with the collar of his shirt, a telltale sign of agitation. So much for quality time. It didn't look like my father and I would make any headway without the presence of my stepmom.

We landed smoothly, and I waited for everybody to exit the plane before grabbing my duffel and following them out.

Julian was waiting next to a large luxury SUV.

"Welcome to Sonoma, my dear friends and guests," he greeted.

"It's a short distance from here to Ambrose Vineyards and Resort, and I cannot wait to show you what we have in store for you," he said.

We loaded into the SUV, and Julian spent the entire ride to the vineyard, chatting our ears off about all the activities they had planned. I, for one, would be happy to just relax, but I was curious to see the place he'd been going on and on about.

As we drove through Sonoma, I looked carefully out the window, sizing everything up and mentally noting places I wanted to check out later. I knew Julian and his business partner had a lot of activities planned for the guests at the resort, but I hoped to sneak away and explore Sonoma a bit on my own. I was seriously considering making the place my home base, and it was the perfect opportunity to get a feel for it.

My good impressions of the place were only strengthened as we rolled up to the front of the vineyard. From my vantage point, I saw the rolling fields of grapevines bursting with grapes. In the distance, to my right, sat a large building that resembled a barn. I assumed that was where they made the wine.

Julian had given me a few bottles of Ambrose Vineyards wines since we'd met each other, and it was damn good stuff. It would be fun to see how it got made. Of course, I'd been interested in the process ever since meeting Paige. The way her eyes had lit up when she'd talked about the science behind it and the subtle art it took to blend the perfect wine ... I hoped she got to work in the industry as she'd wanted.

We stepped out of the SUV one by one. As I got out, Julian rushed to the bottom step leading to the resort's entrance. He turned around with a flourish, welcoming everybody again and assuring us somebody would be along to collect our bags and take them to our rooms. But in the meantime, they would start us with a tour of the facilities.

Julian looked behind him nervously. "Just as soon as my lovely co-host joins us. While I am quite the wine enthusiast, my business partner is the one you should direct questions to about the science behind what we do. She knows the wine business inside and out—I know the bottle inside and out," he said with a wink, and the guests laughed.

Then, a woman came rushing out of the building, smoothing her hand over her hair and down her dress as she did a little jog step to meet up with Julian. "I am so sorry I wasn't here to welcome everyone as soon as you arrived."

Everything in me stilled, except for my racing heart. It couldn't be ...

But as my eyes feasted on the stunning woman standing a few feet from me, taking in her brightly colored sundress and the loose, wavy curls that framed her beautiful face, I had to admit it wasn't some figment of my imagination.

It was her.

"I want to give everyone here the warmest of welcomes. My name is Paige Russell. I'm sure my lovely business partner here already talked your ear off about Ambrose Vineyards and Resort. But I'd love the opportunity to give you a tour of the grounds and answer any questions you may have."

My heart raced to keep up with my mind. Paige. It was my Paige. Our paths had finally crossed again.

PAIGE

And just like that, there was the man who'd haunted my dreams for years ... The one I'd walked away from.

A montage of our night together and the countless fantasies I've had since ran through my mind in a flash.

Still, I must have been standing there with my mouth open because Julian's elbow was suddenly digging into my ribs, reminding me I had a group of people waiting for me. Despite my shock, I plastered on a big smile and forged ahead.

"We are so pleased to have everybody here. If you all would follow me, we'll take a quick tour. And then I'll lead you up to your respective rooms. Dinner will be served at 6:00 p.m. I think you'll love what our chef came up with for your welcome meal."

"Yes, and before we get started on the tour, I want to give a quick thanks to our lovely pilot, Miles, who provided such a smooth flight today," Julian said, applauding Miles. The others turned and followed his lead, giving polite applause.

Miles nodded, but his eyes never left mine.

I sucked in a breath. It all made sense now. Miles had gone after what he'd wanted, just as I had. The realization made me smile, and I met his gaze. How could he still have the same desire in his eyes after all these years? I wasn't the twenty-one-year-old he'd carried into that guesthouse eight years ago.

Before the guests had arrived, I'd put on a quick dab of makeup and brushed my hands through my hair before sliding on my dress and rushing out to be by Julian's side. Fifteen minutes earlier, I'd been rubbing paint off my elbows and hands after doing touch-ups in one of the bathrooms.

A large industrial fan was currently inside the bathroom drying the paint. I hoped to prolong the tour long enough so it would no longer be tacky. Irene, the maid stationed in the room, was making the bed and waiting to ensure the paint was dry before a guest set foot in there.

I made a mental note to add another zero to the bonuses of my staff for their tireless work getting the place together in such a short amount of time.

I needed to pull it together and remember what was at stake—and how hard everyone around me had worked for it. I could not afford to get distracted by a ghost come to life, no matter how gorgeous he was. Apparently, Miles was one of those unfortunate souls who'd aged like ... well, like a fine wine. Go figure.

I waved my hand with a flourish, directing the small group of people to follow me as we wound our way around the vineyard. Once I was talking about what I loved so much, my nerves dissipated, and I fell into the groove of sharing the knowledge I'd worked to cultivate.

Strangely, I found myself focused and even more passionate than usual when I told the guests about my grapes. I could lie to myself and pretend I was trying to buy more time for the paint to dry, but in reality, I wanted to impress Miles.

Despite my desire to show off my knowledge, I carefully averted my gaze from Miles' beautiful dark one. It would be a disaster to give the tour looking only at one person, and if I looked at him for more than a moment, I would fall into those brown eyes just as I had when I was younger, and then I would have no words at all. So, I glanced at him briefly and made concerted eye contact with everyone else, though it frequently brought my attention to the man with Miles, who looked terribly familiar. But for the life of me, I couldn't figure out why.

We worked our way through the winery, where I explained how the wine was made and promoted our classes on picking grapes and learning the fermentation process. Maybe it was my imagination, but for the entire tour, I felt like Miles's eyes were on me.

Don't be silly, Paige. Of course, they're on you. You're the tour guide.

But memories of how he'd looked at me that night came flooding back, and it was like I was a college student again. He was still looking at me like I was the most desirable woman he'd ever seen.

That couldn't be. Surely, he'd moved on. Hell, for all I knew, he was married by now.

That last thought caused a catch in my chest I didn't want to examine too thoroughly.

One guest raised their hand. "Where do we sign up for the classes?"

"Once we're inside the resort, I'll direct you to the front desk, where we have a book for you to sign up for any classes you would like to take."

"Can we sign up for all of them?" A deep voice asked from the back of the group, and then my eyes had no choice but to meet Miles'. I hadn't heard his voice in so long, and the sound sent shivers up my spine as he looked at me, undeterred.

I swallowed hard. "Of course, although don't feel pressure to sign up for all of them—or any of them. If you would like to relax and enjoy the other amenities, we encourage that, too. Please let us know what we can do to make your stay as comfortable as possible," I said, forcing myself to address the entire group as I tore my gaze away from Miles.

I was certain if I looked at him for much longer, the shivers he was inspiring would turn into a full-body orgasm, and that would hardly do in front of the guests, especially the travel blogger. Julian had really done a number on us by sliding that one in.

The travel blogger was frantically taking notes on a small notepad, reminding me of my purpose. It wasn't just my dream I was realizing; my employee's livelihoods were at stake. Julian and I needed to make this work.

The vineyard was successful, but we'd sunk a lot of money into the resort, and we had no choice but to succeed. I would not entertain any other outcome. That meant I needed to keep my eye on the prize.

I led everyone to the pool we'd completed just a few days before.

Although it was thrown together rather quickly, I was proud to show our guests the pool and lounge area. The pool gleamed brightly, with its bright white and blue tiles in a Mediterranean design. Off to the side was a small wading pool with a soothing waterfall feature trickling into its basin.

Opposite the lounge area was a hot tub shrouded by shrubbery and local flowers. Waist-high wrought-iron gates surrounded the entire area, and the landscapers had artfully twined blossoming vines through the iron. After a season or two, you would hardly notice the iron fence, and it would look like a plant wall. It was a beautiful arrangement, and Julian and I had agreed to keep the wall short so guests would have a full view of the vineyard as they lounged.

As the guests looked around the charming lounge area, I allowed myself to take in all the hard work my staff and I had put in the last several months. It wasn't done yet, but we were close, and it would be magnificent. My eyes scanned the property, landing on the man I was trying to avoid. He was watching me again, and when I met his eyes, his intensity softened, and a warm smile spread across his face. God, he was handsome.

I yanked my gaze away, not prepared for the electricity in his eyes. Clearing my throat, I announced, "Now, I imagine you all would like to find your rooms and get settled before dinner. If you would, please follow me this way," I said, leading them to a side entrance that took us to a large foyer featuring several meticulously kept topiaries.

I pointed out some amenities along the way to the elevators and said a silent prayer we would all fit on the elevator together. It was a good thing our other guests were late, although that meant I would have to do the tour again. My nerves were pretty shot after the shock of seeing Miles again.

Thankfully, we all fit into the elevator, but as the doors closed, I realized Miles was sandwiched in right behind me. The smell of his cologne was so familiar, and it flooded my senses. For a moment, I was suspended in time and struggling to believe this was really happening.

Perhaps it was some sort of fever dream after working for too many hours straight.

I wanted to believe that. Only when I glanced over my shoulder, he was looking down at me with expectation in his eyes.

I jerked my eyes back to the elevator doors and breathed a sigh of relief when they slid open. I got out of the elevator like my ass was on fire and tried to compose myself in record time before turning to give a bright smile to my guests.

"We haven't assigned specific rooms. I'll let you choose what works best for you, but I can promise each room is as stunning as the next, with beautiful vineyard views. Of course, there's a phone in each room if you should need to call guest services."

One by one, the guests slipped into rooms, and there didn't seem to be any fuss about who was where. I peered over my shoulder at one of my housekeeping staff, who'd been guarding the room at the end of the hall with wet paint. She gave me a quick nod, indicating it was ready.

When I turned around, Miles was standing in front of me.

I swallowed around the nerves in my throat. "I guess that leaves this room for you," I said, gesturing to a slightly ajar door.

Miles opened his mouth to speak, but a voice came from behind him. "Miles, we need to get a hold of your brother."

When Miles turned toward the man, I slipped away to discuss resort business with Irene, the housekeeper who'd been monitoring Miles' room.

As I walked with her, I glanced behind me and caught Miles watching me carefully.

I grimaced. I was not handling this gracefully, but until I could figure out how to face him without melting into a hot and bothered puddle, I would need to avoid the man.

I remembered our time together fondly, but I had too much on the line to take a walk down memory lane, and it would hardly look professional to my guests to wax nostalgic with an old one-night stand, no matter how gorgeous he was.

As I parted ways with Irene and hurried to my office, I was met with the full force of emotions Miles had inspired. I was struggling to understand why I was reacting this way.

We'd had mind-blowing sex and amazing conversation, but I hardly knew the man. It was just one night. And yet, my heart was racing like I was reunited with the love of my life.

"Maybe Julian is right," I muttered to myself, shuffling through the stack of invoices on my desk. Maybe my response to Miles resulted from working too much and not having more of a social life. I didn't need to date, but I should probably prioritize some self-care time.

"What is Julian right about?" A smooth, deep voice rolled over me.

I waited for a beat, allowing the shivers to rush down my spine before I slowly looked up to see Miles framed in my office doorway.

He grinned widely. "Paige, I can't believe I'm seeing you after all this time."

"Yeah," I huffed out a small laugh. "What are the odds? I didn't know you were Julian's pilot."

"What? He didn't talk about me?" he teased as he stepped into my office. Having him so close made my fingers itch to touch him.

"Well, he has mentioned his pilot, but I hesitate to share what he called you," I admitted.

"Would it be sexy wingman? Or hunky pilot?" he asked with pride.

I laughed. "So, he called you that to your face."

Miles stepped a little closer and said, "Have you ever known Julian to hide anything?"

I shook my head. "No, that's not his style."

"Yeah, he kept telling me about his gorgeous, amazing business partner. I thought all this time he was just talking her up, but I can see now he was holding back," he said, letting his eyes travel from my face down my body. "It's really good to see you, Paige. Better than you know."

I smiled nervously and bit my lip. "Oh, I don't know. I bet you barely even thought of me all these years," I said, looking down at the mess on my desk, babbling out whatever came into my head. "I mean, that was so long ago, and I'm sure you've had plenty of opportunity ..." I was cut off by powerful hands cupping my face, gently forcing me to meet his gaze.

"Paige," he whispered, rubbing the pads of his thumbs over my cheekbones, his eyes going down to my mouth. Then he tilted his head, and before I could utter a single syllable, Miles' luscious lips were on mine.

I was sure my brain must have short-circuited. That was the only reasonable explanation for why I leaned into him like someone had let the air out of me—like I'd been holding my breath for eight years, and the touch of his lips was the first time I'd been able to relax, even for just a moment.

He wasted no time deepening the kiss. I couldn't have stopped the moan that escaped my throat even if I tried. And that moan opened me up to the eager, questing tongue of Miles, who swooped in and tasted me like he belonged there. And God, did it feel like he belonged there.

I wanted to stay in his arms and recapture the thrill of excitement that had enveloped us during our night in the guesthouse. I wanted to chase that excitement to where we stood at that very moment and see where it could go.

Maybe on my desk? Against the back of the office door? Bent over the table in front of my window overlooking the vineyard? The very window I'd stared out many times, wondering what had happened to the man who'd set me on the path to this winery.

In my arms and my mouth was eight years' worth of fantasies and much-loved memories, and yet somehow, I was still being infused with a fresh wave of pleasure and excitement that bordered on scary for how intense it grabbed a hold of my insides.

It was a feeling I could lose myself in—a feeling that would upend everything.

As much as it pained me, that was the moment I decided I would have to push him away. Again.

MILES

Paige tasted even sweeter than I remembered, and that was when I knew I was in trouble.

I'd been trying to make small talk, but when I got close enough to smell her, I couldn't take it anymore. I had to kiss her.

When she sank into me, I snaked my arms around her waist and pulled her flush against me, unable to hold back the moan that ripped from my throat at the feel of her softness against me. It was strange, simultaneously feeling like it had been an eternity since I'd felt her and like no time had passed at all ... like that was where she'd always belonged—in my arms.

My heart leaped in a joyous dance when I heard her moan into the kiss, but our dance was cut short when her hands pressed into my chest, gently pushing me away.

"Miles," she breathed, looking up at me with hazy eyes. But the haze dissipated, and panic set in as she backed away.

"I'm sorry. I'm so sorry. I shouldn't have pushed," I said, hoping I hadn't lost her already, not after finding her after all this time.

But it was the look of dawning in her eyes that brought me back down to earth. My shock at seeing her after all this time had kept me floating behind her during the tour like I was on air. The feel of her lips against mine only made me want more … more of what I probably couldn't have, at least not at that moment.

That crash back into reality reminded me that, in a short amount of time, my little brother and his newly minted fiancée would arrive, and there would be no hiding our relation. Which meant I would have to reveal the years-long secret to Paige only moments after discovering her again.

"Listen, Paige …" I started, but she held up her hand to silence me, and I snapped my mouth shut.

"No, I need you to listen to me," she said softly. "That kiss … was amazing," she said with a small smile. "But as Julian's pilot, I'm sure he filled you in on our situation and that we had to rush to put this together."

I nodded. "He might've mentioned a thing or two about the bind he put you in."

She sighed, running an apprehensive hand down the skirt of her dress. "That's putting it mildly. But we managed to pull it together, and we need to get through this without anyone catching on this was a rush job. Particularly the young woman you saw in the beanie."

"Misty?" I asked. I always made a point of knowing the name of every person who flew on my plane. It was much easier for them to listen to instructions over the intercom if I took the time to actually remember their name.

"That would be the one," Paige nodded. "As much as I would love to catch up with you—because what are the odds we would see each other again—this is a monumental moment, and I need to be the face of professionalism. I can't get caught making out with one of my guests."

"I understand. I'll try to back off while I'm here."

"Try to?" she asked with raised eyebrows.

"You have to admit, Paige, we've still got something. Unless I misread that kiss."

She averted her gaze. "It doesn't matter how I felt about the kiss. What matters is I have a business to run and have had more than enough surprises over the last few weeks," she said, looking pointedly at me.

Something in me soured as I was about to deliver yet another surprise.

"Paige, I don't want to add more to your plate, but there's something I need to tell you …"

"Paige? I'm sorry to interrupt, but it's urgent."

It was the same woman who'd been working in the hallway when Paige was showing everybody to their rooms.

Paige looked at me regretfully and then nodded to the woman. "It's okay. We were just finishing up here." As she moved around the desk, I tracked her movements and how her hips swayed beneath the flowered skirt of her dress.

Her voice jolted me back to reality when she said, "It was nice to see you again, Miles. Please enjoy your stay, and if you need anything, call guest services."

I looked at her face, uncertain. She'd said the words pleasantly enough, and there was nothing inherently wrong with them. But they were coming from a woman I'd just kissed—a woman I knew for a fact was brimming with passion and need. I was being dismissed.

Her face was neutral, and she kept her eyes away from me. I swallowed hard, a sudden surge of sadness rising within me. I bit back a dejected laugh. It had been eight years. A lifetime had happened between now and the last time I'd seen her. Who was I to come in and assume I could unlock what we'd had with one kiss after all that time?

I nodded reluctantly and watched as she excused herself, passing by me.

I would let her tend to her business for now, but the first chance I got, I would have to speak with her about the connection between Leo and myself.

I wasn't looking forward to it, but the Band-Aid needed to be ripped off. Paige had more than enough on her plate, and the last thing I wanted to do was add any more drama to it.

I just hoped the revelation wouldn't soil her memory of us forever.

PAIGE

I rene had been a welcome distraction even if she was bearing unwelcome news. "I'm sorry to tell you this, Paige, but we have a water leak in the lounge."

My eyes widened as I rushed to inspect the damage. She followed behind me. "I hope I didn't interrupt anything with that very handsome guest," she said in a hopeful tone.

"No," I said as I hurried to the lounge. "Why would you think you were interrupting anything?"

"You looked a little flustered ... and he looked a little flustered. Not that I would blame you. You've been working so hard, and he is very attractive," she said with suggestion dripping from her voice.

I huffed out a sigh. "Why is everyone so eager for me to get flustered with somebody, handsome or otherwise?" I found the leak she referenced and bent down to investigate.

"Eager isn't the right word," Irene said. "We just care about you. We see how hard you work. I want you to be happy and have someone to enjoy your happiness with."

"Look, I appreciate that. But what would make me happy at this moment is for this place to operate without incident."

She gave me an encouraging smile. "It will, Paige. We're all in this together. In fact, I already called Julian and told him about the leak. Although, I don't know how much good he'll do."

I rolled my eyes. "Other than to 'survey the situation'? Probably not much. You know him; unless it's the actual tasting of the wine and charming guests, he'll not want to get involved."

I wasn't trying to disparage Julian—I also wasn't saying anything that anyone, including him, didn't already know.

Julian lived a pampered life and wasn't a huge fan of elbow grease. Although I had to give him credit, he'd put in a lot of work for the resort. Just his brand of work involved promotion and getting people interested in visiting. The nuts and bolts weren't in his wheelhouse. Which was why I was surprised when he loomed over me twenty minutes later as I worked a wrench around the leaking pipe.

"I heard we have a bit of a problem," his distinctive voice said. I looked up into the dark shades of Julian's sunglasses.

"I have it under control. We're lucky none of the guests have wandered through the lounge yet."

"Mmm, I see that," he said, looking down at where the puddle had stained my dress.

"I'm surprised to see you here. Irene told me she'd called you, but I figured you wouldn't show up until dinner was supposed to start," I said, walking to the back entrance of the kitchen.

"Ah, well, I'm glad I showed up. It won't do for the guests to see you walking around in a muddy sundress with a big, old, ugly wrench swinging from your hand."

I stopped and glared at him. "Would you prefer they see water spraying from the walls?"

He stopped. "No, that wouldn't do. But while we're on the topic of guests, what did you think of my hunky pilot? Is he a dish or what?"

I gave him a tight smile and then turned to make my way back to the kitchen.

"Is that a yes or no?" he asked. "And it can't be a no. Do you have eyes? You saw him, right?"

"Yes, Julian, I saw him. But that is not what I'm focused on right now."

"I know you're focused on the resort, and while I appreciate that in my business partner, I don't want you to die a shriveled-up, unsatisfied woman."

"Julian, for God's sake, I'm only twenty-nine. You make it sound like I have one foot in the grave."

"Well, you might as well have with the lack of orgasms."

I put the wrench back in my toolbox and then shoved the box back into the maintenance closet, giving him an impatient look. "Do I even want to ask?"

"Everybody knows that lack of regular orgasms leads to premature death. It's good for your heart, it's good for your muscle tone, and it's good for your overall mental health. You have three out of three that you're messing with. I'm not trying to be overly dramatic, Paige. I just worry about your health."

I rolled my eyes. "You want to help my health? Then help me make sure this launch goes smoothly. If we can get through this week and convince our guests this was our intended soft opening date and we didn't throw everything together at the last second, then my health will improve tenfold."

He nodded. "I hear you, I do," he started, which actually meant *I heard you say words, but I didn't actually take in what any of them were.* "But I didn't invite the hunky pilot here with his family just to check out the vineyard. I also invited him to check out the vineyard queen—and let me tell you, I saw how he lit up when he saw you." I scoffed, but he continued, "There were stars in that boy's eyes. It might have been love at first sight," Julian exclaimed, never one to stray away from hyperbole.

"Those weren't stars. That was recognition of someone he once knew," I said before I could stop myself.

Julian's eyebrows shot up. "What? You know the hunky pilot?"

I waved a dismissive hand. "I did. And I certainly didn't know he was your pilot."

"Yes, I did. I mentioned Miles, the hunky pilot."

"No, you only ever referred to him as your hunky pilot. I would've remembered Miles because that was the name of ..." I cut myself off. What the hell was wrong with me? A few minutes with Miles, and I was spilling my guts to everybody? I needed to get a hold of myself. Suddenly, everything was upside down, and I couldn't even handle a simple conversation with my business partner.

"Name of who?" he asked, watching me carefully.

"Nothing, forget I said anything. We have bigger issues to deal with. I need to check on the kitchen to make sure dinner is on track, and then I need to double-check the dining room to make sure the tables are set properly.

"That sounds like a great idea," he said in a monotone voice. "Let me help you."

I laughed at him, "You? Eager to set a table?"

"Not really, but I am eager to hear about who this mysterious Miles once was and how you knew him. So, if I have to sort through cutlery to find out, then so be it."

He wasn't going to let this one go, and while I had no intention of sharing, I wondered if I could dodge his questions long enough to get his help with the table.

I took the gamble. "Fine. Come help me."

Julian gave me a satisfied smile, and suddenly, I wasn't sure I could keep the details from him. He had the gift of gab, and getting secrets out of people that would normally be locked down like Fort Knox was his jam.

I tried to dodge his questions by giving detailed explanations of how I wanted the cutlery folded into the cloth napkins and how each place setting needed to be set out. Julian listened intently, but the second I stopped to take a breath, he jumped in with his questions. "So, how do you know Mr. Miles?"

"It doesn't matter," I said and then gave more directions on the place settings.

"I think it does because I saw the way he looked at you—like he *knew* you."

"Okay. But he doesn't. I haven't seen him in a long time—long before I knew you or even worked at the vineyard. I was still in college."

"College? A hotbed for wild activities. He looked at you a little wildly."

"Now, you're reaching," I sighed.

He hunched down and peered into my face. "No, I'm not." He paused. "I'm not because I see the way your cheeks are turning red, and you won't meet my eyes and ..." He gasped. "Is this the man who gave you the hottest sex you've ever had?"

I looked at him sharply. Was this some kind of voodoo shit?

"Don't you remember?" he asked with a satisfied grin. "A few months ago, we tried that new wine and had a few too many, and you told me all about the passionate night of sex you had at your ex-boyfriend's party?"

"I did?" I was horrified.

"You did," he said and grinned even wider. I pursed my lips together, dismayed by how Julian's smile was turning into a full-fledged jack-o'-lantern.

"I don't remember any such thing," I said, turning my attention back to folding napkins.

"Well, you did," he said in a singsong voice. "Why do you think I've been so pushy about trying to set you up these last few months? Ever since you admitted to me you haven't had anything as hot since that night, I've wanted to fix it for you."

I looked up at his earnest face. "That's actually really sweet of you, Julian," I admitted.

He and I argued a lot, but it was all in love. Julian was like the brother I'd never had. We picked at each other, but I knew he would do just about anything for me—except for general winery chores.

I looked down at his cutlery settings. "That's excellent. You should do this full-time," I said, moving past him.

"Where do you think you're going, young lady?" He rushed after me.

"I need to check in the kitchen and make sure the preparations for dinner are going smoothly."

"You're just going to drop this bombshell and walk away?"

"I didn't drop any bombshell, Julian," I argued. "You guessed correctly."

He smiled again, "Yes I did, go me. But come on, what are the odds my hunky pilot was the guy who gave you the best sex of your life? The guy you admitted to me you still fantasize about."

I turned toward him abruptly, and he had to stop short of running into me. "Julian, I realize it's probably a sordid and interesting story to you. But I need to focus my attention elsewhere. We have too much on the line for me to be distracted by multi-orgasm Miles."

"Oooh, I love that name! That's way better than hunky pilot or sexy wingman. And way to go, Miles," he cheered.

I rolled my eyes again. "As I told Miles, there's too much at stake right now for me to carry on with a guest. Especially with the travel blogger hanging around."

Julian had the good grace to concede my point. "If it makes you feel any better, I've already chatted her up, and I think she's quite charmed by the place so far."

"That's great," I said. "But we have several days to go. I hope the pipe is the worst of it," I said, hoofing my way into the kitchen.

As if on cue, the sous chef came out looking concerned. "Um, I hate to tell you this ..."

"Oh, God," I moaned, hanging my head down. "What now?"

"One of the ovens quit working."

"Shit," I muttered.

"But that means the other oven is still working, right?" Julian asked hopefully.

"Yes, the other one works fine. But it's going to delay the main course because we're going to have to rotate the Cornish hens."

My mind started working overtime, trying to figure out how we could stall the main course before Julian jumped in. "Don't you worry, ladies. I shall entertain our guest until the main course is ready," he assured both of us.

I let out a breath of relief because Julian was great at that. He was great at conversing with anybody, even with the quietest of introverts. I knew he would have the table laughing and talking in no time, and hopefully, they wouldn't notice the main course was a little late.

"While I take care of that, Paige, why don't you go back to your house and rest for a bit before the rest of the crowd gets here," Julian suggested.

"What are you talking about? I have no time to go back and relax," I told him.

Julian rolled his eyes. "Paige, I was trying to be delicate. Look at that stain on your dress. We have more guests arriving any minute now."

My head jerked down to see the very noticeable grease stain on my skirt from messing about with the tools and the busted pipe. "Right, that. Okay, I'll be back in ten minutes," I assured Julian and the sous chef as I backed away from the dining room and rushed toward the kitchen door.

Resting several hundred feet behind the winery was my home. When the Ambroses retired, I wanted them to keep the house. But they thought it best to leave the vineyard altogether and insisted being so close would tempt them to pitch in, and they didn't want to get in my way. Mr. and Mrs. Ambrose assured me Julian and I could manage the place on our own, and it was time for them to pass the torch and leave the beautiful acreage they'd been custodians of for so many years.

They left me with their home, which was a little too much house for me. I would learn later on in my relationship with the Ambroses that when they built the house, they'd hoped to fill the many rooms with their children. Alas, they couldn't have kids, but their family and friends visited often, so the house was rarely empty until I took up residence.

Most of the rooms stayed shut up except for my room and the one that had become Mia's every time she visited.

Sometimes when I let my mind wander, I would imagine what the house would feel like filled up with a family. When I closed my eyes, I could hear the pitter-patter of little feet, and for a few moments, I let myself entertain the notion of how much I wanted that someday. Then, I would shake myself loose of the daydream and remind myself that with no man in sight, it would be impossible to fill this place with children.

As much as I hated to admit it, the daydream would inevitably lead back to Miles and ruminating about the beautiful children we could make together. Never in my wildest dreams did I think he would reappear. I never thought I'd see him again. Maybe that was why it felt safe to fantasize about him. After having no way to find him, there he was, on my turf.

Maybe that was the miracle I had been waiting for? And yet, the timing of his arrival would suggest otherwise.

I rushed through my house and up the stairs to my room, where I quickly skimmed through my closet before finding a slightly dressier sundress than the one I had on. We weren't an evening gown and pearls kind of establishment. I needed something I could trudge around the vineyard in. It was a royal blue dress with white flowers all over it, resembling those Mediterranean tiles from the pool.

I slipped it on and fluffed my hair once more before hurrying back to the resort lobby.

As I rushed toward the door, I saw Irene with a worried expression. Lord, help me. Irene and her worried expressions would be the death of me this week. I was forever grateful for her help, however.

I still didn't know how I got so lucky in rounding up the team of people we had, but they were all more than competent, and we had become a family. They weren't just my employees. They were my friends, and I was so thankful everybody looked out for me.

"Okay, what's the problem now?" I asked.

"No problem. The other guests have arrived, and I wanted to give you a heads up so you would be in tour guide mode by the time you hit the front of the building," she said, falling into step next to me.

I looked at her with a grateful smile. "I really appreciate everything you do around here, Irene."

She nodded. "I've had a lot of different jobs, Paige. I wouldn't want to work anywhere else, even when things are this chaotic."

As we made our way to the front, I quizzed her on the status of the remaining rooms. She assured me everything was ready to go. "Oh, I almost forgot, that gentleman in your office when I came to get you earlier? I ran into him a little while ago. He's eager to talk to you—he said it was important."

I bit my lip, partly out of wanting to hold back my smile and partly as a reminder to calm the hell down. "Thank you for letting me know. I'll find him later," I said as I spied the group by the front steps. I took a deep breath. "It's showtime. "

From my vantage point, I couldn't make out their features, but I saw Julian was approaching them and welcoming them with his usual flair.

I started for the entrance with Irene on my heels when I saw a familiar figure out of the corner of my eye.

Miles.

He was making a beeline toward me, and I gave him a look I hoped conveyed that we could speak later as I directed my attention to the cluster of people standing with Julian.

As I approached, I saw the was group composed of a man and a woman about my age and an older woman. As I drew closer, I realized I knew the man and older woman.

"What's going on here?" I asked quietly to no one in particular, even though Irene answered.

"I'm not sure, Paige. But you look white as a sheet. Are you okay?"

I froze, unsure of what to do and unable to move my feet as I looked at my ex-boyfriend Leo and his mother, Lucy. The young woman wasn't familiar, but now my mind was a mess. What were the odds of running into Miles after all these years and then an ex-boyfriend I hadn't thought about in just as many years?

Just when I thought things couldn't get any more perplexing, I saw Lucy gesture to Miles over Julian's shoulder. She smiled brightly, waving as she hurried up the steps with open arms. I could hear, clear as a bell, as she cried, "Wallace, it's so good to see you, my love."

Wallace? Why did that sound familiar? Wasn't that ...

That was when I heard Leo's voice. It sounded like it was coming from another lifetime as he gently reminded his mother, "He prefers to be called Miles, Mom. He gets ornery when you call him anything else."

That was when it all started clicking together. Wallace was Leo's older brother, or Miles, as he apparently preferred to be called. Holy shit. I'd slept with my ex's older brother.

What. The. Fuck?

Lucy was hugging Miles, and her back was facing me. Miles glanced up, and our eyes locked across the small pavilion. He looked apologetic.

That was when another piece of the puzzle clicked. That is what he'd wanted to warn me about.

This was all too much. I didn't know how to process it all, but I managed to shuffle my feet and move in the opposite direction of the new guests.

Julian's voice stopped me from taking any more steps when he said, "Ah, here is our very own vineyard goddess, as I like to call her. Lucy, Leo, Natalie, I would like you to meet my business partner and the proprietor of Ambrose Vineyards, Paige Russell."

I felt all their eyes on me, and then Leo breathed in surprise. "Paige?"

The woman at his side peered at him with curiosity as Lucy rushed toward me. "Paige?! Is that really you?"

The next thing I knew, I was being bundled into a ferocious bear hug by Lucy.

She pulled back and looked at me. "You are as beautiful as I remember you."

I finally found my voice. "Thank you, Lucy, so are you," I smiled, meaning it. I liked Lucy. Her sons, however, were on my shit list.

She pulled away from me, but her hand was still on my arm as she announced, "Where are my manners? Although I guess Leo should introduce you to Natalie."

"Yeah, Leo, introduce me," the woman said, nudging her elbow into his ribs.

He smiled and said, "Natalie, this is Paige. She and I used to date in college—a long, long time ago," he added. "Paige, this is Natalie, my fiancée." He beamed.

I reached out my hand and shook hers warmly. "It's so nice to meet you, Natalie. Welcome to our resort," I added, remembering myself.

"Yeah, I'm amazed," Leo said. "I mean, you always talked about getting into wine, but I never imagined ..." he said, looking at me, stupefied.

"No, I don't imagine you did," I said confidently.

Okay, Paige, this is the true test. You've been thrown for a loop today, but you can get through this tour. Guests are guests, regardless of your past with them.

I straightened my shoulders and put on my best hostess smile. "Well, if you aren't too tired, I would love to give you a quick tour of the place and show you to your rooms. We'll be serving dinner shortly. I'm sure you must be famished after all the travel."

"You betcha," Lucy said. "I would love to see this beautiful place you've built, Paige."

"To be fair, the winery was here when I took over, but my business partner, Julian and I, have added on little by little ..."

"Or not so little," Julian added, gesturing to the resort behind us.

Lucy and Natalie laughed politely while Leo stared at me in disbelief.

I smiled graciously at Julian, "Well, we've definitely been busy as of late. And we can't wait to share what we've created with you. If you'll follow me this way," I said, steering them toward the vineyard, then watching with dismay as Miles followed along. "Miles ... or Wallace, is it?" I called to him as he gave me a sheepish look. Smiling tightly, I continued, "You've already had this tour. I wouldn't want to bore you with it again." I hoped he would take the hint and stay behind. I didn't want to come across as cold, but good God, I needed him away from me for a hot second.

"You did such a good job the first time. I wouldn't miss going another round," he said.

Julian looked at me as if to ask silently, "What the hell is going on?" I knew the moment we were away from the guests he would be on my case, wanting to hear all the juicy details.

"Of course, the more, the merrier," I said as I turned, leading my new guests to the vineyard. I began with my spiel about how long ago the vineyard had been planted and how the harvest was the perfect season to visit because of the foliage and grape clusters.

I settled back into my normal rhythm of giving the tour, and Lucy, as I remembered her, was ever so gracious, asking me questions with genuine interest. Leo held back, and his fiancée kept eyeing him oddly.

I felt a stab of pity for her. Lord help the woman who got stuck with Leo, especially if he was anything like he used to be. Plus, the last thing any woman wants to do on vacation with her fiancée and his family is to run into one of his old girlfriends, even if there was absolutely nothing left between them.

As bad as I felt for her, the more pressing emotion for me was aggravation with Miles, or Wallace, or whatever the hell his name was. My one-night stand, the man who had been dominating my fantasies for years, who just turned up out of nowhere ... was my ex-boyfriend's brother.

I didn't believe for one second he hadn't known who I was. Suddenly, I had clarity as I remembered the video Lucy had made for Leo's older brother. I remembered Lucy's worry over her stepson's depression and unhappiness with his job. Then I remembered the Miles I'd met at the house party was at a crossroads.

Apparently, he'd decided, as I had, to make a change. And from what Julian told me about his "hunky pilot," he was happy. But why didn't he tell me he was Leo's brother? He had plenty of opportunities that night to speak up.

I couldn't imagine what would've possessed him to keep that from me. It wasn't like I was fawning over Leo when we'd met.

I finished up the tour and was careful to keep my attention off Miles. If I were honest, most of my attention was on Lucy because she was the only thing that made the tour bearable.

I politely showed everybody to their rooms, then rushed away, citing my need to check on the kitchen for dinner.

After escaping the eyes of the guests, I made a beeline back to my office. Down the long hallway to my office, Julian appeared, rubbing his hands together, and I could tell he was brimming with questions. But it must have shown on my face I was upset because his expression sobered immediately, and he stepped in front of me, asking, "Hey, are you okay?"

I looked up at him, embarrassed by the tears brimming in my eyes. *Get ahold of yourself, Paige.*

I shook my head and brushed past him to the office. I needed to get it together before dinner. For some reason, the universe thought it appropriate to throw those two obstacles, or jackasses as it were, my way during one of the biggest moments in my career. I worked tirelessly for the winery, and I was not about to let my past come crashing in and blow up everything.

I rushed to the small bathroom inside my office with Julian right behind me. "Hey, you don't have to tell me any details, but you need to tell me if you're going to be okay. I can make them go away. Whoever is upsetting you," he promised, and I looked up at my friend.

He truly was a good friend. He drove me crazy, but when he saw me upset, he wouldn't care if it hurt our business to throw Miles and his family out.

I shook my head, swiping at my tears. "No. No, that won't be necessary. It's just a weird collision of events. I need to keep it together long enough to get through this soft opening. No man is going to screw it up for me," I vowed, growing more determined with each word that came out of my mouth.

"That's right! We will not let that happen," Julian agreed. "Tell me what I need to do to help you."

I looked at him then, suddenly inspired, and I could feel my mouth break out into a wicked grin. "Here's what we're going to do ..."

Miles

The situation could not get any more fucked up. I wasn't able to warn Paige about Leo's and my connection before my family arrived.

It should have been my top priority, but when she'd looked up at me with those big green eyes and those luscious lips, I couldn't stop myself.

And I didn't regret kissing her, even though it posed an enormous problem for us now.

I'd fantasized about her for so long. It was easy to dream about how amazing someone was when I'd only spent one night with them. I tried to remind myself that if I were to see Paige again, it might not live up to what I remembered.

But when I pulled her into my arms and kissed her, my intuition was right.

It didn't live up to what I remembered—it was better. She tasted even sweeter and felt even better in my arms. Everything in me wanted her more than ever. My desire for her went far beyond a fond memory—it was a fervent need, and if she allowed herself to spend more than two seconds with me, she would feel it, too. That kind of spark happened once in a lifetime—and it didn't happen with just anybody.

But then my stepmother spotted me, and the wheels that had been running in slow motion since I'd landed in Sonoma and at Ambrose Vineyards began picking up the speed of a freight train.

As my stepmother hugged me, I saw Paige's stunned expression.

She knew everything now. And it was made worse by seeing Leo. I doubted she had any love lost for my little brother, but it had to be startling to run into me and then him with his fiancée in one day.

She had to be pissed at me for omitting certain blood relations when we'd met. I needed to explain myself but didn't know where to start. How would I explain she had changed my life before we'd even met? That she gave me hope during a really dark time. How I was hopelessly drawn to her, and I knew my brother was never good enough for her. That I didn't want to scare her away, so I pretended to not know who she was—so I could be close to her.

Eight years ... eight years of pining after her, thinking I'd never see her again, and yet here we are. It was not a coincidence. I wasn't sure what it would take to earn back her trust, but I needed to stop thinking about myself for a moment.

She was under tremendous pressure to make the resort a success, and I dropped a bomb on the festivities when I'd arrived. The least I could do was help defuse the situation. She seemed most concerned about the travel blogger who'd arrived with me.

I'd chartered my fair share of travel writers, and I knew they could make or break a property. It was the same with celebrities. If one celebrity got on social media and complained about a place they'd stayed at, the place was as good as dead. It was apparent how much Julian and Paige had worked on their resort, but knowing Julian, it was probably Paige's elbow grease that got the place to where it was.

I headed toward the lounge to see if I could find Misty and assess the situation. Perhaps I could positively influence her opinion. That was when I noticed a water leak coming from the wet bar in the lounge. I might not be able to mend things with Paige, but I could fix that.

As I marched into the resort lobby, I nearly ran into the maid who'd interrupted Paige and me earlier. I think Paige had called her Irene.

"Irene?"

She smiled in recognition. "Yes, sir, how can I help you?"

I gave her a hesitant smile. "I know this is an odd request, but may I borrow a wrench?"

"A wrench?" she asked, her brow bunching in confusion.

"Yes," I said simply. "I'm assuming you have a maintenance closet around here somewhere. If you would point me in the right direction, I'm sure I can find what I need."

"Oh, um, sir?" she said, flustered as I began moving toward where I suspected the closet might be. "Is there something wrong, sir? I assure you our staff can handle whatever requires a wrench," she said, following frantically behind me.

"Where is it? In the kitchen?" I asked, going toward the kitchen.

"Miles!" I heard a friendly but suspicious voice behind me. I turned to see Julian smiling at me with questions in his eyes. "Do we have a problem?"

"The gentleman says he needs a ... wrench?"

Julian's eyes widened. "What on earth would you need with a wrench, my dear Miles?"

I stepped closer to him and said, "There's a water leak in the lounge. I thought I would take care of it before anyone saw it."

Julian's smile dropped. "Oh God, the leak started again. Paige was just working on it. We thought she'd fixed it. Do you think you can fix it with nobody noticing? Especially Paige?" he asked hopefully.

I nodded. For Paige, I would do anything. "Point me toward the tools."

Julian looked around as if he would be caught at any moment before leading me to a hallway that took us through the kitchen to the maintenance closet. Grabbing a tool bag, I made my way back to the source of the problem. It wasn't too difficult to fix. My guess was it needed a bit more manpower behind it. I knew Paige was strong, but she was a lot smaller than I was, and I could put the extra weight behind getting it shut off and sealed.

"That's outstanding, Miles. I cannot thank you enough," Julian said as I finished cleaning everything up.

"That should hold for now. But you'll probably want to get an actual plumber to look at this after we're gone."

"I will add it to the list, and ..." Julian's voice trailed off, and I looked up, blinded by what was left of the sun. "Paige!" Julian said. "I thought you were still in your office."

"What's going on here?" Paige asked, and I could tell she was in no mood for games.

Time to take it like a man. I wanted to have a conversation with her, and this was my opportunity. "I noticed a water leak and wanted to take care of it before anyone saw," I said, rising from my crouching position.

"That really wasn't necessary. Besides, you're a guest here. You shouldn't be worrying about ..."

"Paige, it's fine. I wanted to. Julian has been telling me for a while about all the hard work you have been putting into getting the resort ready. I want it to be successful for you."

She narrowed her eyes at me. "Is that the only reason, Miles?"

Throughout our exchange, Julian looked back and forth between us like he was watching a tennis match, with glee dancing in his eyes. I looked at him and asked, "Julian, would it be okay if I had a couple of minutes to talk to Paige? Alone?" I added when I saw he was still planted firmly in his spot.

He smiled. "Of course, of course, I'll be right over here," he said, pointing to some ambiguous spot over my shoulder.

Once I was sure he was out of sight, I stepped closer to Paige. "Look, I'm sorry if I stepped on your toes. I just want to help. I know how important this is to you and Julian, and yeah, I would like to start making up for ... well, everything."

Her lips pursed before she said coolly, "Are you referring to the fact you knew I was your little brother's ex-girlfriend the night we slept together? Or that you failed to mention it at any point?"

I scrubbed a hand over my face. "Yeah, that. Listen, I know fixing a leaky pipe doesn't even begin to make up for my lapse in judgment. Truth be told, there was this beautiful woman in front of me, and I wanted so badly to spend more time with her, and it seemed like a buzz kill to say, 'Hey, by the way, that dude you wasted your time with, I'm his older brother.'"

She rolled her eyes. "Regardless of how much of a mood killer it might've been, it was still pertinent information, don't you think?"

I shrugged helplessly. "You're right. I messed up, and I'm sorry. I should've said something. That was what I was trying to tell you when I got here, but ..."

"But things kept happening," she filled in.

"Right. And Paige, I'm still in shock it's you Julian's been talking about all this time. I never thought I'd see you again."

Her expression softened. "Me neither. I've wondered what happened to you quite a few times," she admitted.

"Really? I wondered about you all the damn time," I said with a laugh. "I can't tell you how many times I kicked myself for agreeing to us being a one night thing. It changed everything for me."

I was about to tell her everything I'd held inside me for eight years. How the video of her encouraging me helped me through the most challenging time of my life and then how holding her in my arms had given me the strength and courage to change my life for the better. I just wanted to spill it all, but I didn't want to risk scaring her away.

And yet, I couldn't stop myself from stepping closer, inhaling her sweet scent, falling into those emerald eyes that were looking at me with such ... was that longing? Because it certainly looked a lot like what I was feeling.

I reached out and brushed my fingertips over her cheekbone. Her lips parted on a sharp inhale. "Paige ..." I started as I bent down farther, but she shook her head and stepped back.

"I'm sorry, Miles, I can't. As nice as it is to go down memory lane ..." She turned away to leave but whirled back around to face me again. "You shouldn't have lied to me! I can't wrap my head around the fact you're Leo's brother. And I'm really pissed you knew who I was and never told me! But more than anything, I don't have time to sort it out right now. So, please, let me get back to work. Thank you for your help, but I don't need it."

Before I could get a word out, she turned and rushed away. In a matter of moments, I felt like the guy who'd run away to his parents' lake house—dejected, confused, and hopeless.

I must've looked like it, too, because I nearly jumped out of my skin when I felt a hand clasp my shoulder. "Don't give up, big guy," Julian said.

"I thought you went inside."

He smiled coyly. "I went inside-ish." I rolled my eyes, but Julian was undeterred. "I don't know the details of what's going on between you and Paige, but I wouldn't give up hope."

"You wouldn't?"

"Nope." He looked thoughtful for a moment like he was about to say something else, but then his face paled. "I would, however, stay out of her way when she has that look on her face," he said, motioning his head forward.

My gaze snapped around, and there was Paige, eyeing us both with determination. "Julian, it's time for dinner," she called with more than a little edge in her voice.

"Coming, dear!" he replied. I snickered as he said, "That means you, too. Just remember what I said."

I kept Julian's words in my head throughout dinner, even though the last thing I wanted to do was steer clear of Paige.

She showed up to dinner looking gorgeous, as always. I couldn't take my eyes off her as she and Julian worked the table masterfully. I shouldn't have been surprised she'd grown into such a capable, confident woman. Despite the stress of opening a new resort and the chaos created by my family's arrival, that night was the first time I experienced how much she loved what she did.

If there was any tension between her and Leo, she didn't show it. My brother, on the other hand, seemed a little uncomfortable. Poor Natalie kept asking him if he was okay. He would nod as he continued to stare at Paige with a perplexed look.

I tried to make small talk with my father, who was seated next to me, but as usual, he was surly and said very little, except for the passing comment, "That hostess is a looker."

"Walter, don't you remember? She used to date Leo," my stepmom pointed out, but my father just grunted.

My father was unlikely to remember any woman either of his sons had dated. Even when they came to the house to meet the family, my father always locked himself away in the office or spent his time responding to messages on his phone. As far as he'd been concerned, they were one and the same, and he frequently mixed up their names. He'd called Natalie Stacey or Shelly on more than one occasion.

To Natalie's credit, according to my stepmother, she'd hung in there and smiled graciously through those awkward exchanges. I hadn't been around all that much. In the last several years, I'd been too busy flying. My father was still perturbed with me for leaving the practice and loath to admit I was successful in doing something he didn't approve of.

"Hmm," my father said. "Maybe Wallace can have her."

My stepmom swatted at his arm. "Walter," she said in a chiding tone.

"You're talking about a grown woman, not some doll to be passed around. Although she is darling, and you two would make a cute couple, Wallace."

I smiled at her tightly. "Thanks, Mom, but I'm not looking right now."

That was a bald-faced lie. But if I admitted that to her, it would force me to answer questions I didn't yet have the answer to—or maybe I did, but I was afraid to say it out loud for fear of jinxing it.

The woman of my dreams was sitting at the end of the table. And she wanted nothing to do with me because I'd lied to her. I'd had sex with my little brother's ex-girlfriend and didn't tell her who I was. She may never forgive me—served me right.

When I turned away from my father, my eyes met Paige's from across the table. Our gazes held for an extended moment, and there was that longing again. I would give anything for the people around us to disappear, leaving Paige and me alone to see if what we had all those years ago could be recreated.

I tried to play it cool as dinner wound down. I loathed the moment I would have to walk away from Paige, and I knew sleep would not be coming for me that night.

After dinner, we moved to the lounge for a nightcap, and I made small talk with my family and the other guests—keeping an eye on Paige.

She mingled for a while, but I noticed she kept making her way closer to the exit at the back of the room. The sun had gone down, and I'd gotten to watch a beautiful sunset behind the fine-boned shoulders of the woman I'd been dreaming about for what felt like an eternity. In the hazy light that stretched across the dusky sky, the flyaways of her hair almost looked like a halo.

But there was nothing angelic or pure about what I wanted to do to Paige, and more than once when our eyes met, it felt like a wild collision of our deepest inner thoughts before she would break the gaze and smile or laugh at something somebody said.

But after the sun went down and the guests paired off, enjoying their glasses of Ambrose Vineyards wine, I caught Paige looking over the group of people with a satisfied grin on her face as she slipped down a short staircase at the back of the room.

I wound my way around the room to see where she went off to, and that was when I noticed the house nestled in the vineyard. I'd seen the rooftop many times when I'd flown Julian and other guests to the winery, but I'd never put two and two together until now. It had to be her house, where she laid her head every night.

The intense urge to see the inside of that place, to see where she slept and what her shelter away from expectations and work looked like, was overwhelming. I wanted to experience what Paige did after a long day of work, how she unwound. And I desperately wanted to be with her in that house.

She'd admitted she thought of me over the years, and I hoped she fantasized about our night together as much as I had.

Once I could no longer see her shadow, I excused myself and made my way up to bed, but as I suspected, sleep evaded me.

The rooms were luxurious, and I had to credit Paige for her attention to detail. The rooms resembled something one might find in an Italian villa, complete with a small balcony I stepped onto.

My eyes roved over the vineyard, the moon illuminating the property as if it were daytime. It was a beautiful place—I could see what drew Paige here. I stepped back into my room and permitted myself to lie down, though I knew visions of Paige would plague my mind.

I couldn't fight it for very long, and soon, my hand wandered down to choke my erection. I fondled myself briskly, giving in to the urges that had taken over since I'd seen her face again. Nothing was satisfying about the way I pleasured myself. It was almost punishment, squeezing and stroking, bordering on painful. Gritting my teeth against the agony of having to take care of my own orgasm when I knew her sweet mouth, and even sweeter pussy, were a short distance away.

I came hard with a feral growl of frustration.

Something had to be done—I had to get closer.

PAIGE

I was exhausted. I should have fallen asleep before my head hit the pillow, but I slept for all five minutes before my eyes popped open, and I remembered the insanity of the past forty-eight hours. Little did I know the stressful preparations for that week would pale in comparison to the appearance of not one but two ghosts from my past.

The ghosts I'd thought had absolutely nothing to do with one another—other than they were both at the lake house on the same night—were brothers.

What fresh hell brought this on?

Despite all the shenanigans, we made it through the first day. Only a few more to go. And if I could hold it together, then we would get through it with a bang.

Everybody was happy and satisfied when I'd left the lounge after dinner … well, everybody except for Miles, whose gaze had followed me all evening. He kept as far away as he could, but I was deeply troubled by how he looked at me—and I was even more troubled by how turned on I was.

He looked at me just as he did eight years earlier, and that delighted me. I couldn't believe he was still so enamored. Perhaps that wouldn't be the case if he got to know me as the woman I was now. But at the moment, Miles seemed more than convinced that fate had brought us together again.

I wasn't sure I believed that. Then again, I always thought it was fate I met the Ambroses. It felt meant to be that Julian and I had bonded and teamed up to take over the vineyard. So, was it really that outlandish to believe fate would bring Miles back to me?

"This is absurd. I have to get some sleep," I muttered, throwing my covers back and trudging into my bathroom. I dug through my medicine cabinet until I found my melatonin gummies, hoping they would save the night.

I had no time to be tossing and turning over Miles.

I needed to remain focused—and I had to get the way Miles had looked at me out of my head.

I looked at the clock again. Though tempted to head into the resort an hour ago, I'd forced myself to stay put until my usual start time. The longer I was in the building, the more things I'd found that needed to be fixed, and the more I fretted over it.

The opening staff had assured me that if anything went wrong, they would call or text me, and so far, my phone had remained blissfully silent. But the silence made me nervous.

"Get a hold of yourself, girl. That means everything's going okay. Take it as a win," I coached myself as I did my hair and tried to cover the dark circles beneath my eyes.

At my normally appointed time, I left the house and strolled toward the lobby. In another forty-five minutes, breakfast would be served, and then the guests would go about their business until that afternoon when a wine-tasting class would take place.

I used to teach the classes, but since we'd expanded and I'd been pulled into so many directions, we'd hired a talented sommelier who came with glowing references. Greta was a lucky find. She could've worked at any fine dining restaurant of her choosing, including big cities, but she'd been looking for a slower pace and decided Sonoma would be a good fit for her. When Greta took over the classes, I could direct my attention to more pressing resort matters, and I couldn't be more grateful. It seemed like every thirty seconds, a new fire emerged that I had to put out.

Thankfully, with the bulk of the guests at the wine-tasting class, my staff and I would have time to fine-tune any issues that had popped up.

As I walked down the hall, I heard a banging noise. "Oh, no, what's that?" I asked as I hurried down the hall to the kitchen.

When I burst through the kitchen door, I discovered our hard-working chef, Martha, being comforted by Julian.

If Julian was there this early, I knew something had to be wrong.

"What's going on? Julian, why are you here so early?"

He gave me a reassuring smile, although it didn't have the desired effect. "I told the staff if they needed anything this morning to call me because you need rest. You've been running yourself ragged."

Though it touched my heart, I also found it extremely irritating. "Julian, that's insane. I'm right here on the premises. If I'm needed, they should call me."

"Yes, my darling, but it was brought to my attention last night how hard you worked putting this place together, and it got me thinking I have not been pulling my weight. So, I informed the staff to let you sleep in today. For all the good that did, you're still here early."

The banging started again, yanking my attention toward the back of the kitchen. "Why is the freezer door open? And what is that banging?"

"I came downstairs this morning to prepare breakfast, and half of the freezer contents have thawed," Chef Martha explained.

"Oh, my God. How much did we lose?"

"Breakfast is pastries, so we're fine there, but all my ingredients for lunch and dinner didn't make it," she said miserably.

"Shit," I cursed.

"I told you we should've gotten new freezers, Paige. I was always suspicious of those used ones," Julian said.

"We didn't have the budget for brand new ones. They've been working great until now. No sign of an issue."

"She's right. I thought we got them for a steal until I came down this morning," Martha confirmed.

I let out a long breath. "Okay, breakfast is still on track. But we have to come up with a solution for lunch and dinner. I can slip away to the supermarket this morning and ..."

"Oh, no, no, no," Martha cut in. "I have certain standards I adhere to. I made that very clear when I started working here. Supermarket produce will never touch my kitchen counters. Only the best comes out of this kitchen."

I sucked in a cleansing breath through my nose, trying to stay calm. "But the farmers' market isn't open today, Martha. The supermarket is the only option."

Martha's face turned beet red. "We must find another option because that simply won't do," she said, throwing down the tea towel she'd been worrying with her hands as she huffed off.

My eyes met Julian's, and he shrugged as if to say, *What are you gonna do?* And I had to admit, he was right.

We adored Martha, and she'd become a part of our family, but she was persnickety about her ingredients. I supposed that was what made her food so delectable, but at that moment, I needed her to dial it down and lower her standards. Besides, the supermarket wasn't that bad—at least, it wasn't as bad as she claimed.

I sighed. "Let me call our suppliers and see if they'll do an emergency run," I said, exasperated, as I turned and heard the banging again. "At least you got the repairman out here already. Thank you for that, Julian."

"Oh, I didn't have to call a repairman. One sort of popped up and offered to help," he said with a nervous smile as I approached the pair of legs sticking out from the table that butted up against the side of the freezer.

"What do you mean, one popped up?"

That was when the body scooted out, and Miles's head popped out from under the table. "Miles?!"

He gave me a wide grin. "At your service."

"What are you doing under there? Are you even qualified to do that?"

"Well, I'm not completely sure. But I have to tinker with the engine on my plane pretty regularly—how different can they be? There's a fan on the side, and it looks like the belt wore out. Plus, it could use some more coolant. I can grab some in town," he said as if he talked about freezer motors every day of his life.

"Miles, I told you I don't need your help ..."

He nodded. "And I heard you, Paige, but Julian needed my help. He and I are pals, so what kind of friend would I be if I told him no?"

"Well, to be fair, you offered," Julian spoke up from behind me. "And he is fixing it, Paige, so I believe the proper expression is, thank you," he said, moving up beside me and jabbing a bony elbow into my ribs.

I jumped at his movement and offered Miles a resigned smile. "Thank you, Miles." As the smile on Miles's face faded, I had a pang of remorse for the coolness in my tone, but I wouldn't let that stop me.

I whirled around and headed back to the front desk to make my phone call. I needed to get that supplier on the line and see what it would take for them to do an emergency run to the vineyard. And the guilt I felt for pushing Miles away had to stop. I'd been clear with him about not having the capacity to process seeing him again right then. I didn't have time for him to make it up to me, and I didn't have time for the feelings that danced inside my chest every time he smiled. And I certainly didn't have time for the throbbing pulse he inspired between my thighs.

I could hear footsteps behind me as I walked. "Paige," he called behind me.

I turned to face him. "Look, I'm sorry if I sounded harsh; it's just that I don't want you to think that helping around here will make up for a lie that stretched years."

"And how do you know I wouldn't have told you the very next day if you'd have stayed?"

That made me stop. "Would you have?"

"Honestly? I don't know what I would've done, but I can't change the past. What I know is I desperately wanted you to stay."

"That wasn't what we agreed to," I said quietly.

"I know. I'd hoped that after the night we shared, you would change your mind ..."

"Part of me wanted to stay, Miles, but I felt like I needed to figure things out on my own. I had already given up so much for a man, and I was afraid ..." I stopped myself and shook my head. "It doesn't matter. What matters is I have people counting on me, and I need to see this through."

"Which is why I want to help you. That's all I want to do. None of this is to make up for anything. I've done what I've done, and I can't take it back. But I will tell you this—I'm not that confused guy anymore. I've done a lot of growing up. In fact, nothing about me is the same except that I still want you," he said in a low voice, stepping closer to me.

I looked up into his dark eyes, and my heart quickened when his eyes fell to my mouth. I wished to God I hadn't let him kiss me the day before because then I might have a shot in hell of being able to resist him. I could still taste him on my lips and feel his body pressed against mine, and it drove me insane. The night before, in my sleep-deprived brain, I'd fantasized about how good it would feel to have him inside me again. And from the look in his eyes, it appeared he'd been thinking the same thing.

The vineyard was still officially closed for another thirty minutes, so nobody was manning the front desk. But a guest could still wander downstairs at any moment and catch me as I was about to kiss another guest. I knew, without a doubt, that if our lips touched again, there would be nothing chaste about it, and if I was lucky, I might wind up with my legs wrapped around his waist and him backing me up to the front desk.

He tilted his head and lowered his mouth to mine. A rush of air fanned over my lips as he breathed, "Paige."

I balled my hands into fists by my side, giving one last ditch effort at reprimanding myself to be professional, but the throbbing in my pussy was too intense, and I was certain all the blood had left my brain.

That was when the front doors swung open with a heavily accented voice bellowing, "Guten Morgen! We're here." The last two words were sung out.

I whirled around to see a familiar face in a not-so-familiar get-up. The woman in front of me swung her long blonde mane over her shoulder. "Oh, I'm so sorry," she said, digging her elbow into the man beside her. "It looks like we interrupted."

I smiled at her. "Of course not. Welcome to Ambrose Vineyards."

"Oh, don't be silly, dear. We've obviously interrupted. It's okay. Nothing wrong with a little early morning schnitzel," she said in her over-the-top accent.

I glanced over my shoulder at Miles, who was eyeing the new guests curiously.

"Nonsense," I said with a forced laugh. "He was just leaving."

He looked at me, disappointed, and said, "Oh, sure. I'll let you take care of these two," as he reluctantly shuffled away.

I tried to calm the racing of my heart and waited until Miles was out of sight to turn around and ask in a hushed voice, "What's with the accent?"

Mia grinned at me. "You said I needed to be in disguise, so ol' what's-his-face wouldn't recognize me. I thought I'd add a little flare to it," she said in her normal voice. "What do you think of my new blonde locks? I'm trying the Barbie look," she said, flipping the trusses of her blonde wig back.

"I think they're very becoming," Danny said. "Although if it's okay with you, I'm not doing an accent. My German is horrible, and we would be outed like that," he said, snapping his fingers together.

I eyed my two aces in the hole. They were the plan Julian and I had cooked up the day before. I called Mia, cashing in every favor she owed me by asking her to stay for the week as a mole.

The only snag was Leo might recognize her, although they'd spent very little time together when we were dating. When I expressed my concerns to Mia, she assured me I needn't worry about that. She'd done PR for countless businesses over the years and had accumulated tons of swag, including a few wigs from a company that sold them along with hair extensions.

Every once in a while, when we would go out for a girl's night, she would put on a new wig and try out a "new personality." I'd met that personality before, but I didn't expect her presence at the vineyard. "Ursula Von Der Horst at your service," she said, bowing.

"Oh, my lord," I muttered to myself.

"Yes, and I am her *very* straight husband, Brock," Danny supplied.

"Brock?"

"Yes," he nodded. "That sounds like the name of a man who has sweet, sweet, heterosexual sex with his wife every night and not like a man who did filthy things to Julian last night." Danny smiled and winked.

I made a face. "TMI, Danny."

He tsked at me. "I am no longer Danny, young lady. I am Brock—remember that."

I smiled at them. "Right, Ursula and Brock," I confirmed, then let out a relieved breath and told them earnestly, "I can't thank you both enough for doing this."

Mia waved off a dismissive hand. "Don't mention it. I've been needing a break, and this is the perfect excuse. For the next few days, I don't have to think about PR campaigns or dumb stunts my clients have pulled and trying to do damage control. I can relax in a beautiful resort and pretend to be somebody else for a while. I think it'll be fun."

"Me, too," Danny agreed. "Although it will be hard to pretend not to be attracted to Julian ..." he said, looking down at Mia with mischief in his eyes. "We could pretend like we're looking for a third for a threesome, and I rope in one of the hotel owners."

I cleared my throat to get their attention. "Might I remind you of the plan to talk up the resort, not to star in your own soap opera?"

"Party pooper," Mia sighed. "And that's certainly rich coming from you, considering we walked in here about to catch you making out with some hot guy. Who was that? Tell me everything."

I stiffened. "Listen, I can't get into it now, but that was Miles."

Mia's mouth dropped open. "As in the Miles who gave you the best night of your life that I've been hearing about for entirely too long? That guy?"

I nodded and leaned forward, whispering. "Yes, it is the same Miles, and it turns out he is Leo's older half brother."

Danny and Mia gasped audibly. "Shut up," Mia said in a stage whisper.

"Listen, whatever you think you need to do right now, it can wait. You have to fill me in on what the hell is going on. I knew you sounded strange when you asked for help, but never in my wildest ..."

"Oh, this is juicy," Danny interrupted, clapping his hands together. "I want in on this conversation, too."

I sucked in a deep breath. "Look, I'll give you guys all the details, but I can't right now."

Mia tilted her head, looking at me speculatively. "Don't you have to give all the new guests a tour?" she asked, and I caught her drift. That would buy us some time for me to fill them in.

I sighed. "Fine, but let me call my supplier first, and then I'll do the tour."

The supplier said the earliest he could get me something was for the evening meal. I ran to Chef Martha with the news, and she offered to make something from the leftovers from last night's dinner and give it a fresh spin for lunch. That would have to do. We had little choice because she was adamant about no supermarket.

I hurried back to the front desk to meet up with Mia and Danny, and we were about to head out the door when a voice called out behind us. "Paige?" I turned around to see Misty, the travel blogger, racing to catch up with us. "Are you going on another tour? Is it okay if I tag along?" She had a camera around her neck and a phone in her hand. "I didn't have a chance to take pictures yesterday and was hoping I could tag along, maybe film parts of the tour, if you're okay with that, and the new guests, of course," she said, smiling to Mia and Danny.

"Oh, I don't think ..."

Mia cut me off in her heavy German accent. "Of course! We'd love that! Allow me to introduce myself. I am Ursula Von Der Horst, and this is Brock ..." She trailed off, looking at Danny with a raised eyebrow.

Danny smiled and stuck out his hand toward Misty. "Just Brock, you know, like Cher."

Misty nodded and shook their hands. "Well, it's nice to meet you, Ursula and just Brock. Would you mind being included in the tour video? I have a couple million followers, so if you're looking to get some publicity, this will only add to it."

Mia gasped. "Oh, we live for publicity." That was no lie.

As a group, we headed toward the vineyard, and Mia took the reins and chatted Misty's ear off, raving about every stop on the tour. Misty asked more in-depth questions about what it took to maintain the vineyard and how long the vines had been there while filming on her phone.

As we returned to the resort, Misty stopped to take some pictures with the Nikon strapped around her neck, and Danny helped stage certain shots for her as Mia pulled me to the side. "Well?"

"You two are doing wonderfully. I cannot thank you enough. I just feel bad. Not only did I drag you away from your life, but now I'm asking you both to lie."

Mia rolled her eyes. "As we say in PR, it's not a lie; it's embellishing the truth. Nothing I said about the vineyard was a lie. It's just the accent I said them in, and that's all. And besides, I like Ursula. I think I'm going to enjoy being her for the next several days. But don't think I'm letting you off the hook for spilling the tea about Miles. Is this the part where I high-five you for hitting two brothers?" she said with a slow grin.

"Eww. I haven't even thought of it that way."

"Oh, come on, if the genders were reversed, dudes would congratulate each other into the ground for bagging two sisters."

I shook my head. "It's not that simple. He could've told me. I've spent all these years thinking about this wonderful guy I got to spend an amazing night with, and I come to find out he lied from the moment he met me."

Mia nodded. "That is a bummer. Although when you think about it, it is a bit of a buzzkill to say 'Hi, by the way, I share DNA with your crappy ex-boyfriend.' Which reminds me, how is ol' Leo? Still as weasily as ever?"

I shook my head. "He's just some guy. It was weird. I mean, I remember dating him, but it's like I don't know him, and it's hard to believe I pinned all of my hopes on him at one time. He brought his fiancée, and she seems really sweet."

"Bless her, she probably doesn't know what she's gotten into," Mia said, but then Misty and Danny were walking back toward us, and Mia straightened. I could visibly see her morph back into "Ursula."

"This all looks so wonderful, Paige," Misty enthused. "Everything has been spectacular since I got here, and I meant to tell you last night how wonderful dinner was. I would love to talk to your chef whenever they have a moment. I'm excited to see what they come up with for lunch."

I gave her a wide smile. "Me, too," I said, trying to tamp down the nervous ball threatening to launch itself into my throat.

"Well, feel free to explore the grounds, and I hope we'll see you at the wine-tasting class this afternoon," I told them. We said our goodbyes, and as soon as I walked away, I could overhear Danny telling Misty, "Have you seen the amazing pool? I was here when they broke ground. It is gorgeous. Did you know the tiles were flown in straight from Athens?"

The hell they were, but well done, Danny.

When I was certain they were out of sight, I rushed back to the kitchen. I was going to help Martha in any way I could with lunch, and I prayed to God she came up with something palatable for the meal. She was a sorceress with food, so I had to trust she had it covered.

An instant wave of her relief washed over me when I walked into the kitchen and saw the prep table brimming with produce and other ingredients.

The kitchen staff was chopping and blending things into bowls and shoving things into the oven. The sight did my heart good, but everything in me stilled when I saw Miles sticking out like a sore thumb. Chef Martha was hovering over him with encouraging words. "That's good, but let's try the julienne cut. Here, let me show you," she said, taking the knife out of his hand and doing a quick chop on a pepper.

I watched as he followed Martha's instructions and felt the smile creeping across my lips when Martha clapped as if she were encouraging a child. "Magnificent, Miles. Now, if you can do that on four more, that would be perfecto," she said, patting him on the back and turning to answer a question from the sous chef.

I stepped farther into the kitchen until I was across the table from him. "I hate to interrupt," I started and grimaced when he nearly sliced off the tip of his finger. "Sorry, I didn't mean to startle you."

He looked at me with a modest smile. "It's your kitchen, Paige. I'm just trying to help."

"I see that, and I'm surprised Martha actually let you in here to touch her food. She's normally very protective."

Miles locked eyes with mine, his grin stretching his lips as he winked at me. The man actually winked at me. My mind began to over-analyze how I should feel about it, but my body was quick to understand as tendrils of excitement raced down to my crotch.

"Well, you may be immune to my charms, but Martha's not," he said in a low voice.

I shook my head at him, rolling my eyes. "Humble much?" I asked as I looked down and wondered about all the produce. "I guess the supplier surprised me by getting here early?"

Martha turned, then smiled with a satisfied expression. "No, our dear, dear Miles, here got a hold of the farmers' market vendor and talked him into selling to us today. Isn't that wonderful?" Martha enthused before turning back to her dish.

Miles smiled. "It's no problem, really," he said, staring down at his hands as he cut up the rest of the peppers.

Martha looked down in horror at what Miles was doing with the peppers. She faked a smile as she said in gratitude, "That's quite enough with the peppers, Miles. Thank you. In fact, you've been a great help, but we're good here," Martha said, pushing him out of the kitchen and away from the mangled peppers.

I bit back a laugh as Miles was dismissed, then led him out of the kitchen. "Listen, I realize I haven't been the most receptive to your help, but I appreciate what you've done. I don't know how you managed to get ahold of the vendors on an off day. They're usually too busy in the fields to bother with anybody."

"Yeah, well, between you and me, that was a little white lie I told Martha to get her to take the food."

I could feel my brow furrow. "Where exactly did it come from?"

He bit back his smile. "The supermarket," he drew out. "I got rid of the bags, brought everything in baskets, and rinsed them off really well, and she didn't know the difference."

My eyes widened. "Wow, just wow," I said in delighted shock. "She can never know, you hear me?" I said in all seriousness.

He nodded. "Hey, I just spent the last thirty minutes watching her wield knives. She won't hear anything from me. It'll be our little secret."

I had to fight back a laugh, knowing all too well what kind of hell would rain down on Miles's head if Martha found out her precious ingredients had come from the "tainted supermarket."

"What will be your little secret?" a voice asked from behind us, and Miles and I turned to find Leo looking between us suspiciously.

Miles swallowed hard and said, "Nothing, just a little joke I played on the chef."

"It's never a good idea to mess with the people who make your food, Miles," he said before turning to me. "Paige, I meant to tell you last night how good it was to see you. This is quite impressive," he told me, not quite meeting my eyes." He shoved his hands into his pockets, which I remembered was his nervous gesture. It was funny. I hadn't thought about that in so long, yet it all came rushing back. "My fiancée is a real big wine drinker, so she's loving it here. "

"Good," I answered. "I hope you two will make the wine-tasting classes. Anyone who loves wine really gets into our classes, and our sommelier is fabulous."

Leo smiled, still not meeting my eyes. "Good. Great. I'll make sure we're there. Well, I need to get back to Natalie to make sure Mom's not overwhelming her with wedding details." With that, he nodded and wandered away.

Miles looked down at me, and I shrugged in answer to his silent question. "Does it make you uncomfortable to have him here? You two didn't exactly end on the best terms," he said.

I shook my head. "No. That was so long ago. I feel like a completely different person, and I'm sure he is, too," I offered, wanting to give him the benefit of the doubt. "He's just somebody I used to know; that's all." And it was the truth. The breakup with Leo hurt like hell at the moment. But it hadn't taken me long afterward to realize it was the best thing that could've happened to me. He and I weren't right for one another, and once I was free of him, I felt a new confidence to go after what I wanted.

"Is that what I am to you, too?" he asked quietly.

My smile dropped. "Miles ..." I started, but he held up a hand to stop me. "I'm sorry," he shook his head. "I said I wouldn't push, and here I am doing just that."

"No worries," I said, biting my lip to keep myself from saying everything else I wanted to tell him—like how much I thought about him, how I couldn't stop thinking about that kiss, and how I craved his touch.

But I didn't say that. Instead, I gave him a polite nod and excused myself.

Once I was out of eyesight, I hurried away. I needed to put more space between us because when I was that close to him, I could literally feel my self-control slipping through my fingers. Seeing the two brothers next to each other should remind me why I need to keep my distance. Knowing Miles was a part of that family complicated things.

I remembered the tense relationship Leo had with his father, and I remembered hearing about how it affected his older brother. Even though it didn't bother me anymore, I remembered a lot of the hangups Leo had when we were together, and I couldn't help but wonder if Miles had those, too. All the resort stuff aside, I had to question if I would be setting myself up for failure by getting involved with Miles.

"Cool your jets, Paige," I reprimanded myself.

There was no point in stressing about a potential future that may never be. In a few days, Miles, along with his family, would be gone, and I would still be here, right where I started.

Except I was determined not to be back where I'd started. In a few days, I hoped there would be glowing reviews from all my guests, jumpstarting our new resort. I needed to quit living in the past and mulling over what was. I needed to stay present and focus on the most important week of my life ... and stay the hell away from the mesmerizing Miles and his tempting lips.

MILES

I took the stairs to get back to my room. I needed to walk this off—the angst, the aching. Paige was going to drive me insane. Every time I got close to her, I couldn't help but have a physical reaction, and I knew she had the same response, but damn if she wasn't stubborn. The best I could do was try to help her get through the week and hope I wasn't crossing any lines.

Although I had to admit that going into the kitchen and offering food to Chef Martha felt good. The kitchen staff was so excited, and they welcomed me with open arms. I enjoyed being with them, just as I enjoyed being around everybody at Ambrose Vineyards. It felt like family, like Julian and Paige had built a little village, and it added to the appeal of Sonoma.

Driving into Sonoma that morning to secure the groceries, I'd had time to explore a bit. I got to walk around and talk to a few of the residents, and it further confirmed my suspicion it would be a great place to live. Of course, the town could be on fire, and I still would've been sold on living here, knowing Paige was nearby.

I was in the middle of unlocking my door when my stepmom's voice sounded down the hall. "Oh, there you are, Wallace. I've been looking all over for you."

"What's up, Mom? Is Dad okay?" I asked, starting toward her.

"Oh, he's surly and cranky, so yes, he's perfectly normal. Don't worry. But I was thinking, since everybody would be doing the wine-tasting class this afternoon and your dad's not interested, maybe you and he could do something together."

I smiled at her. My stepmom had done her best to be the peacekeeper over the years, and I knew none of us had made it easy for her. She had the patience of a saint—and the persistence of one as well.

To be honest, her pleas have fallen on deaf ears for a long time until recently. I remembered getting that phone call several weeks ago about Dad being in the hospital.

I'd completed my charter flight as fast as humanly possible and raced home to be with him. And that was when we got the news he didn't have much time left.

I hated the memory of holding my stepmom as she'd cried into my shoulder. My father had insisted we not say anything to Leo or Natalie. Leo had been in the middle of a high-profile make-or-break case, and he didn't want him to have any distractions.

Leo had recently won that case, but as far as I knew, neither my dad nor stepmom had revealed anything to him. He was their baby. They had a habit of protecting him like that.

"That sounds great, Mom. I'll see if maybe he's up for some golf or something," I promised her.

For years, I'd carried a lot of resentment for how my dad and stepmom had babied Leo while I'd been fed to the wolves. I'd made peace with that once I quit law, but I still felt a lot of bitterness from my father about leaving the family practice—no matter how much I loved what I was doing now. I'd pushed all those feelings aside when I saw him looking so vulnerable and weak in that hospital bed.

My father was an old dog, and he wasn't likely to change. I loved him, and that was what I needed to focus on, not all the things I wished he'd done or said to me. It was important to get as much time with him as I could, even though it was hard to get close to my dad. I'd hoped the trip would make it easier for me to spend some time with him without him grumbling about what I could've done with my life.

"Oh good! Thank you, Wallace. He'll enjoy that. And it looks like you've been enjoying yourself since we've gotten here. I saw you talking up our hostess."

"You mean Leo's ex-girlfriend?" I reminded her.

She shook her head. "Oh, they were babies when they dated. They're two grown people with two separate lives now. Leo is with Natalie, and they're happy. I want my other son to be happy, too, and I can tell you from firsthand experience that Paige is amazing. I always knew whoever was lucky enough to win her heart would get the best wife."

I nodded with a smile. The last thing my stepmom needed to do was sell me on Paige. I was already sold lock, stock, and barrel. But I wasn't about to share any of that information with her.

If my stepmother had any idea what had been going on in my head since my arrival at Ambrose Vineyards, she would already have wedding plans and names picked out for our future children.

Never mind the fact my presence put Paige on edge. The last thing I needed was my well-intended stepmom to exacerbate the situation. And Leo acted awkward as hell around her. I couldn't help but wonder if maybe he'd finally realized how badly he'd messed up.

That made me feel bad for Natalie because she was a nice woman and seemed well-suited for Leo, but there was something about how he behaved around Paige when he'd discovered us at the front of the resort earlier. While I knew he'd been affected, it made me realize how far Leo and I had drifted apart because I had no clue what was in his head or heart.

As lucky as I felt to have found Paige again, I needed to remember why I had agreed to take this week at the resort with my family in the first place—to spend as much time with my father as possible and to mend fences with my brother.

The doctor told my father that while the spot he found on his lung was operable, he would still need chemo and possibly radiation. When my parents flew back to Los Angeles the following week, they would spend one night at home and then go in for my father's surgery. We wouldn't know more about his prognosis until then, but the doctor had speculated that with the size of the tumor, it was likely Dad only had a few months to live.

I'd beaten myself up on and off since seeing him in the hospital because I hadn't encouraged him to quit smoking sooner. He hadn't dropped the cigarettes until I graduated from high school, but that was after decades, and it finally caught up with him.

My regrets ate at me as I waited in the foyer for my dad to appear. No sooner had I wondered where he was that he appeared in his khakis and polo shirt, the official golf uniform.

"Are you ready to tee up?" I asked him.

He grunted his typical response but seemed more relaxed now that we were escaping the wine-tasting class. "It'll be nice to get out on the green," he said gruffly. "If I have to hear one more thing about table settings or how many guests are going to be at Leo and what's-her-name's wedding, I might kick off right here."

"Dad ..." I reprimanded in a light tone.

"What? I don't see what the big deal is. Just do the damn thing and be done with it. You kids make such a big deal out of everything these days," he groused.

I shook my head. There was no convincing my dad, and I didn't want to bother. I didn't want to spend the little time we had left together arguing over stupid things. We'd wasted enough of our life doing that.

My dad and I waited outside near the front steps for a rideshare to appear, drinking in the warm sun and the vineyard. That was when movement caught my eye.

I squinted and craned my neck to catch the movement again, making out the weave of a sun hat bobbing up and down in one of the rows of vines. It was Paige.

She had a clipboard in one hand while the other inspected the grapes. I wasn't sure what her process was, but she methodically worked her way through the vines, giving me a chance to just watch her. She was so relaxed in the vineyard as opposed to the tension she exhibited while in the throes of trying to hold the resort operations together. She played it cool in front of the other guests, but I could sense how important the winery was to her.

A nondescript sedan rolled up, and my father approached the rear door. As he got himself seated and I walked around to the other side, Paige looked up, and our eyes met.

We stood there for a long moment, staring at one another, and that all too familiar band of longing clenched around my chest. Maybe I should've waved and smiled, but in the end, I tore my gaze away and got into the backseat of the car at the urging of my father. "Are we going to play or what?"

On the ride to the golf course, my father was surprisingly animated as he bragged about his latest golf score, and he then gave me several unhelpful tips on how to improve my game. I smiled and nodded in the right places and tried to concentrate on what he was saying, but my mind wandered to that melancholy look on Paige's face.

She clearly had her act together, but for some reason, she was unwilling to show any vulnerability except for that one moment. At that moment, I could see longing and maybe even a little loneliness.

Paige was longing for much more than just the rush of professional success. She was longing for someone to hold her and love her. And while she wouldn't admit it, we both know it could be me if she'd allow it.

PAIGE

After all the near misses Miles and I had over the last couple of days, why was his gaze full of longing the thing that kept me tossing and turning? It wasn't like the memory of his touch and the taste of him still on my lips wasn't enough to keep me from sleeping, but it was that look of ... hope. It was so full of something that tugged at my heart and had me tossing back the covers, pacing the floor next to my bed.

Miles distracted me to no end. Knowing he was nearby, pulled my attention elsewhere.

When I did a tour with the guests, I wondered if Miles was nearby. If I stopped in the hall to talk to one of my staff, I wondered if he was watching me. When I walked into the kitchen to check on meal preparation, I wondered if he'd been in to chat with Chef Martha or if she had successfully banished him from the kitchen.

It was so distracting and created a bittersweet ache, lodging itself in my chest, near my heart. On countless occasions since our night together, I'd managed to convince myself it was a one time thing. But being around him again made my heart race and made me question all the grim pragmatism I'd used when trying to convince myself that what we shared could never extend into the real world.

"This is ridiculous," I muttered as I pulled on an old pair of pajama shorts and slipped on my gardening boots. Between that and the sleep shirt draping down my thighs, I was sure I must have looked ridiculous. But it didn't matter. No one would see me where I was going.

When I was stressed out or feeling alone in the world and unable to sleep, I would go to the vineyard and commune with the vines. As silly as it sounded, those grapes knew all my secrets. It was quiet and peaceful, and there was something about the damp earth beneath my feet and the fragrant smell of the grape clusters that instantly calmed me.

Unfortunately, even the vineyard couldn't quiet my thoughts tonight or keep my brain from racing back to the hopeful eyes of Miles.

"What are you doing to me, Miles?" I quietly asked the still night air.

"I don't know. Why don't you tell me?" I jumped out of my skin at the response.

I whirled around to see Miles, standing tall and broad between the vines—he was a fantasy come to life. All those nights I'd walked the vines fantasizing about him, and now, here he was, mere inches from my touch.

I opened my mouth to say something, anything, but nothing would come. What could I say that hadn't already been said? It sounded like a broken record, even to my ears.

I didn't know if it was the moonlight shining down over Miles, lighting his face and revealing to me the heat and desire in his eyes. Maybe it was because we were standing in my favorite spot in the entire world. Or maybe it was the sweet smell of the grapes on the vines assailing my nose, but I was so exhausted keeping it all together I just didn't have it in me anymore.

So, I reached for him. Running my hands up his tight abdomen and over his chest, curling them around his neck and urging him down. He didn't need convincing. His lips were on mine immediately, but Miles wasn't the one taking charge. I pulled him flush against me, twining my arms around his neck and forcing my tongue between his lips. A growl escaped his throat when I tasted him.

What led to us stripping our clothes off in the middle of the vine-yard was still a blur. I knew that one moment I was kissing him as if I needed him for air, and the next, my gardening boots were gone, my baggy pajama bottoms were off along with my t-shirt, and the warm night air was caressing my naked body as he laid me down onto the hard-packed earth.

So many things were similar to the first time we were together, yet it was an entirely new experience. I wasn't some young woman fresh off a breakup, trying to discover herself again. I was a grown woman who'd been dreaming of reuniting with this man for years. It almost felt like a hallucination, the way he shoved himself between my thighs, kissing me urgently as his hands played my body like an instrument, torturing the areas that longed for him the most. Plucking my nipples, making my back bow against him, and then slipping them inside my honeyed depths and making me gasp against his mouth.

"You have no idea how long I've dreamed about this ... how bad I have it for you," he whispered against my lips. The intensity in his eyes made me believe he meant what he said, but he was wrong. Because I, too, knew what it was like to long for somebody for eight years—to wonder what would've happened if I had stayed.

"Miles, please," I pleaded. I needed him as close to me as possible. I needed to feel him, to know, without a doubt, that he was finally with me again.

He seemed to understand my urgent need. The moonlight framing his shoulders allowed me to watch the way his muscles flinched as he slowly pushed his thick, hard-on inside me.

I let out a relieved cry of joy. I must have been smiling because when he looked down, I could see a smile tugging at the corner of his lips.

He was still for a moment, just watching me. "Please, Miles," I urged, needing to feel his movements, and he replied by leaning down to rest on his forearms, looking into my eyes as he started moving. He made eye contact the whole time. I wanted more of him—I needed all of him.

Pleasure wracked my body, and I reveled in the sight of sweat glistening on his skin. My eyes followed the beads of sweat to where our bodies became one.

He was gritting his teeth, and I knew he was holding back for me, but he didn't have to wait long because my orgasm was barreling down on me at a speed that both frightened and exhilarated me.

My hands grasped at his back, and he must've been able to tell I was getting close because he started encouraging me, "That's it, Paige. Let me feel that sweet pussy squeeze my cock. Come for me."

His words liberated my orgasm as I screamed out into the vines. Miles's climax followed behind mine, and he buried his mouth into my neck, muffling his own shout of release.

My long-held and cherished memory of that bewitching night on the lake had quickly become overshadowed by a tryst in the vineyard beneath the moon, staring into the eyes of the man I'd been dreaming about for eight long years, the man I still couldn't quite believe was here.

We laid in each other's arms, and I reveled in how his heart thudded against mine—like our heartbeats were in sync.

Holding him in my arms and staring up into the night sky with the stars twinkling down on us, all my excuses for pushing him away didn't make sense anymore. None of the things I'd been worried about mattered anymore. It was just him and me, the stars and the vines.

MILES

There was no way I would let her go now. Not when we'd proven that what we'd shared all those years ago wasn't a fluke. There was something real, raw, and undeniable between us, and it could no longer be ignored.

Our time in the vineyard was quiet, aside from our moans and groans of pleasure. When I came down from our first orgasm together, we rested in one another's arms for a while until I pulled back and looked into her eyes—I would steal every moment I could with her that night.

I disentangled myself from her arms and lowered myself to rest my mouth on her pussy. I'd been starved for eight years, and I was finally going to get to drink the nectar that had given me life for so long.

After several more orgasms, the sun began to rise, and I cradled her in my arms and whispered in her ear, "Tomorrow night, Paige, I'll come to you. Promise you'll let me in."

I steeled myself for what I knew could be another rebuttal. Another reminder of why she couldn't do this right now—why we would be a bad idea because all the reasons.

Instead, when I looked into her eyes, she didn't argue. She simply nodded, and I helped her get dressed before we walked hand-in-hand out of the row of vines. I walked her back to her house, and when we got to her door, she turned around and rose on her tiptoes, giving me a sweet kiss before whispering, "Sweet dreams, Miles."

And then she disappeared into her house like some sort of ethereal vision.

After a few hours of sleep, I woke with a stupid grin, wondering if last night had really happened. I would have questioned it myself if it wasn't for all the aches and pains I had from rolling around on the ground all night. I didn't care, though. It was worth it. I felt like a teenager again sneaking to her house that same night, and I was grateful for the comfort of her bed, even though we got little sleep. Our night was spent exploring with less haste. I tasted every inch of her, and her lips touched every inch of me, and I delighted in all the sighs and moans that slipped from her throat.

We didn't discuss our future; we just enjoyed one another.

Once again, we found ourselves on her front porch as the sun came up, and as she was kissing me goodbye, my heart soared when she asked, "I'll see you tonight?"

I nodded enthusiastically, and she bit her lip, holding back a laugh. "What?"

She shook her head. "Nothing, it's nothing. I just think it's funny we had one night together eight years ago, and now, here I am, nearing thirty, and I feel just like I did when I was twenty-one. It's like we got in a time machine or something."

I smiled at her and gave her a long, lingering kiss before releasing her. "It's not a time machine, Paige. It's our reality now," I told her, enjoying how she watched me as I backed away.

I would return to the resort and enjoy a few hours of sleep. As tired as I was, it didn't bother me. I was living off something much more powerful than sleep. Little did I know it was about to come crashing down.

Later that morning, after I enjoyed a late breakfast, I spied my family in the lounge area around the pool. My dad was in one of the lounge chairs, reading a thriller, and my stepmom was sitting at the edge of the pool, her feet dangling in the water. Natalie laid out sunbathing in a chair on the opposite side.

"Where's Leo?" I asked the assembled family members.

My stepmom looked up to speak, then hesitated.

"I'm right here, you sorry son of a bitch," Leo ground out behind me.

I turned to him in confusion. "What's your problem?"

I barely got the last syllable out before Leo's fist came soaring toward my face. Luckily, I dodged him, but he rocked forward and pitched into the pool.

My stepmom let out a squawk, and Natalie rushed from her lounge chair to Leo.

Leo came up sputtering, fury in his eyes.

"Do you want to tell me what the hell this is about?" I asked him, walking to the pool and offering my hand to help him out.

But he pushed my attempts to help away. "Don't act like you don't know. I heard you this morning with your girlfriend—you know, the one who used to be mine? The one who you were apparently sleeping with at the same time as me."

My brow furrowed deeply. "I'm not sure what you think you heard, but you've got it all wrong."

Leo grabbed onto the side of the pool and shoved himself onto the edge. "Oh, do I? Was I mistaken when I heard you talk about how you spent the night together when she was twenty-one, which would've been when we were together?" he spit out.

I shook my head, not wanting to get into this in front of the whole family. "Look, man, you need to calm down, and then we can talk about this—privately."

"I don't want to calm down, and what's the point of being private about it? You've been making such a big deal about the family getting closer together this week, so let's involve everybody. No secrets, right?"

I shook my head, resisting the urge to deck him.

"Now, what the hell is this about? Aren't you two a little old to be fighting over a girl? And aren't you marrying this one?" my dad said, motioning toward Natalie, rising from his chair and coming to stand in between us.

"Look, nothing scandalous happened," I started, but Leo would not let me off the hook. He was all in now.

"Are you fucking kidding me? You don't call having sex with your little brother's girlfriend scandalous? I might believe she did it to get back at me, but I don't understand what the hell I did to you."

Frustrated, I spit out, "She wasn't your girlfriend anymore. It was after you broke up with her, and she didn't even know I was your brother. Not until she saw us here."

"You lying sack of ..."

"Boys, that's enough. Can't you see you're upsetting your mother?" my dad said, looking at both of us sternly, his face growing redder by the second.

"You don't understand, Dad," Leo started, but he wouldn't finish because my dad suddenly grabbed his chest and fell to his knees.

"Walter!" my stepmother cried out, rushing over.

I dropped to my knees as my dad collapsed to his side. "Dad? Dad, talk to me. What's going on?"

We huddled around my dad, trying to figure out what the hell was happening, and the next thing I knew, almost all the guests were surrounding us. My dad's eyes were still open, but they didn't seem to see any of us, and he wasn't responding.

"What's going on?" I heard Paige's voice behind me.

"He collapsed. He's not responding, Paige," Ursula, the guest who'd arrived late and was now speaking in an American accent, said.

Behind me, I could hear Paige barking out orders, and then she was kneeling beside me, talking to my father. In a calm voice, she said, "Mr. Townsend, please stay with us. We're getting you help. Can you hear me?"

My father's eyes closed. He'd passed out, and Leo was moaning, "Oh, God, please."

My brain kept telling me to move, but I was frozen. Paige wasn't. She pushed both me and Leo to the side and started doing chest compressions, counting off before doing mouth-to-mouth. Over her actions, I could hear my stepmother praying loudly to not take him yet. The chest compressions went on forever, although in reality, it was only a minute before my dad's eyes popped open, and he gasped for breath.

A murmur of relief went through the crowd. And somebody announced, "Thank goodness, the ambulance is here."

Everything became a whirlwind then. One moment, I was looking into my dad's eyes as he clutched my hand, and the next, he was being carried away on a stretcher.

I hadn't noticed Julian show up, but he was ready with an SUV, hurrying my family in.

As the SUV pulled away, Paige waved to me from the stairs, concern etched into her features. I wanted to roll down the window and tell her to get in with me, but I knew it wasn't the time.

How did this morning, which started so exquisitely, turn out like this? I wasn't ready to face the music. I wasn't ready to lose my father, and now it felt like I might lose my brother, too.

PAIGE

I checked my phone for what felt like the hundredth time in a few minutes.

"Don't worry, I'm sure he'll get in touch just as soon as he knows anything," Julian reassured me, patting me on the back.

"What the hell just happened?" I kept asking. Mia filled me in about the very vocal argument between Leo and Miles and how their father tried to break it up.

I shook my head in disbelief. "Why the fuck would he care after all these years? He has a lovely fiancée, and he and I were not good together, so what does it matter?"

"It's a sibling thing," Danny interjected. "Especially with brothers. There's always an element of competition, and even though Leo may not want you anymore, now he's interested because Miles is playing with his toy," he said.

I shook my head, still in disbelief. I didn't understand any of it, but then again, I was an only child, so obviously, this is above my pay grade.

"That's so stupid. I remember Leo was always impulsive, but to make a scene in front of the whole family ..." I grumbled.

"Well, not just the whole family, more like most of the resort guests," Julian said with a grimace.

My eyes shot to his. "Seriously?"

He nodded miserably. "I don't mean to sound uncouth, and I do worry about poor Miles and his family, but we may have a bit of a mess to clean up here."

I let out a long sigh. Out of habit, my mind chewed on the fact that everything we'd worked for was probably ruined, but for the first time—that wasn't my utmost concern.

Come on, Miles, let me know you're okay. I couldn't imagine what he was going through. Mr. Townsend had always been a grump, but Lucy adored him. For what it was worth, I sensed the feeling was mutual, but Walter wasn't known for wearing his heart on his sleeve. I supposed that was what made him excel as a lawyer.

"Paige?" Irene called from the office doorway. "They're ready," she said.

I sighed, "Here we go. Wish me luck." I had arranged for a staff meeting to address this morning's fiasco, but as I marched toward the front desk, Misty, the travel blogger, intercepted me.

"I'm afraid I'm going to have to wrap up my stay a little early. It's obvious you have more than enough going on here, and I've seen everything I need to see," she said.

I bit my tongue, fighting the urge to talk her into staying. There was no point in pleading with her because the last thing I needed was to come across as desperate. That would be even more embarrassing, considering what had transpired today.

"Well, I certainly hope you think of us the next time you're in Sonoma," I said, trying to remain upbeat.

Her eyes widened. "Oh, I won't forget this place," she said with a laugh. "I'll send you a copy of the pictures I took and give you advance notice when the blog post goes live."

"Thank you. Let us know if there's anything else we can do."

She nodded and then went on her way.

When I turned around, I jumped when I realized how close Julian was.

"How do you do that?" I asked.

"Would you say she was upset? Or just that she had another engagement she needed to get to?" he asked hopefully.

I shook my head. "I honestly don't know, Julian. This whole day has been a nightmare, and there's not much we can do. We tried our best, and now, we move forward."

"Well, I think that's a healthy way to look at it. The resort isn't everything, and it's not like we won't have more chances to make it shine. But I have to ask, is what Leo accused Miles of true? Have you two been ... canoodling?"

I narrowed my eyes at him. "I'm not answering that question," I said, striding away.

He followed close behind me. "I'm not trying to mettle in your affairs or press for details ... although, when things have calmed down, I would love those details. But, Paige, there is clearly something between you and Miles. And you're worried. You don't worry about anybody. Do you see a future with him?"

I sighed. "I don't know, Julian. When I'm with him, I feel amazing, and ... it's all-consuming, and it scares me."

He looked at me, confused. "Well, that sounds wonderful. Why does it scare you?"

"I'm scared by how I feel when I'm around him—scared it will consume me, and I'll lose sight of my goals and dreams. I'm scared I'll turn back into that submissive little doormat who lived her life for somebody else and not herself."

Julian's eyebrow rose. "At the risk of overstepping—but fuck it because, next to Mia, I'm your best friend, so I'm going to overstep now—I think you're scared of more than that."

He moved closer to me, his voice kind as he explained, "Paige, I've watched you turn this place into your world, and it's the most beautiful world. But you've done it to the exclusion of a romantic relationship. This place is wonderful, and I am so happy to be a part of it with you, but it can't be everything you need. I'm wondering if you throw yourself into work because you're afraid of getting hurt again."

I shook my head, looking away from him. "That's ridiculous."

"Is it, though? This place can't hurt you like a man can—or has. I know you agree Leo was not the one, and you understand why, but that doesn't mean he didn't hurt you, and it doesn't mean the pain hasn't stayed with you. It hurts being rejected—it hurts being made to feel like you're not enough."

I rolled my eyes. "I've hardly been heartbroken for Leo for all these years," I huffed out a laugh.

"No, but maybe you've been heartbroken over Miles. But before he had the chance to hurt you, you went ahead and did it for him. You told yourself all the reasons it couldn't work out to protect yourself. I think some part of you knows that what you have with Miles is epic, and you're terrified of what it might do to you if it doesn't work out."

I gawked at Julian, who was looking at me kindly. I didn't know what to say. It was a lot to take in, and every word struck exactly where Julian aimed—and I was angry with him for it.

So, I responded the way I usually did when someone got too close to the truth of my emotions. I stuck my nose in the air and announced, "I don't have time for this. I need to do damage control." And I stomped away from him before he could say another word.

Except I didn't do damage control. I locked myself in my office and checked my phone every few minutes, willing Miles to let me know he was okay. And all the seconds in between those minutes, I thought about what Julian had said. I thought about everything I felt for Miles: the passion, the joy, the longing ... the love.

MILES

The next few hours were tedious.

Upon arriving at the hospital, the medical team checked out my father carefully, and it was determined he would need emergency surgery. There would be no waiting until he was back in Los Angeles. It would need to happen now.

Everything happened so fast, yet the wait was so long. I sat in the waiting room trying to console my stepmother as Leo and Natalie wandered off to the hallway, where I could hear them bickering.

I knew exactly what they were talking about. Leo had revealed a lot just before my dad collapsed. It had to be terribly confusing for Natalie. I knew the ins and outs of my fractured relationship with my brother and the years of competition that led to that moment, but she was just beginning to understand it—and Paige had unknowingly played a role.

In the meantime, I listened to my stepmother's worries, and I worried right along with her. Then I thought about Paige—as she was never far from my mind. The last time I was in the hospital with my father, I'd already been thinking about slowing down the pace of my life. But knowing he only had a few months to live made me face the fact that nothing was guaranteed, and sometimes in life, we had to jump without a safety net. I'd never felt that more keenly than I did in that waiting room, holding my stepmother's hand.

When Leo returned, Natalie wasn't with him, but I didn't dare ask where she was. It wasn't the moment. He sat down in the hard plastic chair across from us, putting his head in his hands and looking like he'd just run afoul a field with land mines. Nobody said anything for a long time. Our tense silence was only ended by the arrival of Dad's doctor.

We all stood in anticipation of what he might say, and his expression could only be described as ... baffled?

"Well, folks, I have to say, in all my years practicing medicine, I've never quite seen anything like this. First of all, the diagnosis he received a few months ago was incorrect. Mr. Townsend never had a tumor."

We all looked at each other, dumbfounded.

"But the doctors back home seem so certain," my stepmom told the doctor.

Dr. Richmond was nodding. "I can see why they came to that conclusion. The lung scan shows a considerable mass in your husband's lungs. However, when we opened him up, we discovered it wasn't a tumor, but histoplasmosis."

"Histoplas what?" Leo asked.

"Histoplasmosis," Dr. Richmond said again. "It's a lung infection caused by breathing in fungus spores. We breathe them into our bodies all the time, and most of the time, we don't get sick. Your dad is one of those unfortunate souls whose body could not combat it on his own. We've put him on a course of anti-fungal medications, and he should be good as new in a few weeks. He needs to watch his stress levels, however, because that will only hinder the healing process."

"This is insane," I said in shock.

Dr. Richmond nodded. "It's definitely one for the books. But this is good news. He doesn't have cancer, and as long as he watches his diet and manages his stress, he has a long life ahead of him."

My stepmother let out a relieved sob, and then she couldn't stop. I brought her to my chest, and Leo put his arm around us as we hugged. There was a chorus of "Oh, my Gods" and "Thank God's" coming from our little group until my stepmom popped her head out and asked, "When can we see him?"

"Only one at a time, but I can take you to him now, Mrs. Townsend," Dr. Richmond said.

My stepmother extricated herself from our embrace and sprang to Dr. Richmond's side, asking question after question as they hurried down the hall.

That left Leo and me alone. He looked at me, relieved. "Wow, can you believe that?"

I shook my head. "We got lucky."

He nodded in agreement and moved away, pacing and running his hand through his hair. "Look, Miles, we need to talk about earlier."

I held up my hands. "We really don't. So much has happened today ..."

"I know. That's why I think it's important we talk now," he said.

He was so adamant that I relented, sitting back down in the waiting room chair. Leo plopped down into the chair across from me, and I waited for him to speak. I didn't know what I expected to come out of his mouth, but it was definitely not what followed. "I want to apologize to you for being so upset earlier. It was a long time ago, and Paige and I were broken up. I didn't have any claim to her, so if you two spent a night together and connected, that's none of my business, even if it is *really* hard to wrap my brain around. And if you've connected again, and she makes you happy, then I'm happy for you," he said, having a hard time meeting my eyes.

"Why does it bother you so much? You have Natalie, and she's wonderful. Why did it bother you at all? Do you still have feelings for Paige?" I asked.

Leo shook his head. "It's stupid, really. I don't have feelings for Paige anymore. Not that she's not great, because she is. But there's a reason we broke up. We weren't right for one another. When we broke up, I was such a dick, and I've regretted that for years—how I handled the situation and how awful I was to her. When I saw her again after all these years, she reminded me of what an ass I was back then. It wasn't until I met Natalie that I wanted to change and be a better man. Being reminded of who I used to be is humiliating," he admitted. "But that's kind of the point, right? I need to accept I can't change the past, and I will continue to run into people I've wronged. Like Natalie said, the best I can do is try to make amends and show them the man I am now."

I nodded slowly. "That's very wise. I saw her rushing out of here. Are things okay between the two of you?"

Leo nodded. "I hit the jackpot with her. She was upset and confused by the whole situation at the pool. She was certain I was lying about this old girlfriend, but when I told her what was going on, she knew I was telling her the truth. She's been with me on this whole 'trying to be a better guy' journey—a guy worthy of someone like her. I fucked up today, and I was most definitely not worthy of her."

"Not every day will be perfect," I reminded him. "You make the choice to do your best every day and let the rest fall away."

He nodded. "That's what Natalie told me. She rushed out of here because she felt like we should be together, just the immediate family. Plus, she wanted to make arrangements to ensure Mom and Dad have extra help at the house while he's recovering and it's fully stocked before they get home."

"That's kind of her."

He nodded. "That's Natalie. She's pretty amazing."

He slapped his knees with finality and then rose from his seat. "After I visit with Dad, I'm going to head back to the resort and help Natalie. Then, I need to track down Paige and apologize for how I treated her. She probably doesn't give a shit about what happened in college, but it needs to be done."

"I'm sure she'll appreciate it," I said.

Leo looked hesitant before he said, "You really care about her, don't you? I mean, I don't want to pry, but I saw the two of you on her porch, and it's obvious there's something undeniable between the two of you."

I nodded. "I love her," I admitted. "I think I've loved her for eight years."

Leo's eyebrows rose in surprise. "Wow."

I nodded in agreement.

"Dude, does she know you feel this way?"

I laughed. "It's hard to imagine she doesn't if you've seen how I follow her around like a puppy, but I haven't said the words if that's what you're asking."

He looked at me thoughtfully. "Paige is pretty smart, but she's been burned in the past, and you have me to thank for that. Make sure you actually say the words, make sure she understands how you feel, hold nothing back."

I nodded. "Since when do I get relationship advice from my little brother?"

He chuckled. "I have become quite wise ... through my proficiency at jackassery," he said, as he turned to head down the hall toward our dad's room.

I laughed behind him, feeling at peace for the first time in a long time. I mended my relationship with my brother. My dad would not expire in a matter of months. And fate brought me my dream girl.

Now, I needed to make that fantasy my permanent reality.

Shortly thereafter, Leo and I headed back to the resort.

We saw our dad briefly, but he was out of it, and the nurse didn't want us to tire him out. My mom stayed, of course, but Leo and I left so as not to be in the way.

As soon as we got back to the resort, I made a beeline for Paige. I knew this time of day she was probably in her office. When I came upon her office door, it was ajar, and I could hear her and Julian talking.

Julian said, "You need to quit being so hard on yourself, Paige. It's all going to work out."

I heard her sigh and then say, "It's easy for you to say, Julian. You have something to fall back on." She said something in between, but I couldn't make it out, and then, "I wish you hadn't brought Miles and his family here. It's been such chaos."

It felt like somebody had shoved a knife into my chest, and I bit my lip to hold back the grunt of pain her words caused.

I knew we'd been an inconvenience. I knew she hadn't been expecting any of it. But after the nights we'd spent together and all the deep conversations ... for her to say she wished we'd never been here? That took the wind out of me and damn near made me fall to my knees.

It was as if Paige and I had been having two completely different experiences. She'd been the one pushing me away, keeping me at bay. I was the one who kept pursuing and insisting it was fate.

Now, I would be the one to crash into the brick wall of reality.

She didn't feel the same way I did. That was clear now. Maybe she gave into my pursuit out of loneliness, but what I heard in her voice through the gap of her office door was easy enough to understand.

I'd read the situation completely wrong. I'd found the love of my life after eight long years, and in a matter of days, I lost her, too.

Paige

Oddly enough, it wasn't Miles who updated me about the situation with Mr. Townsend.

Natalie found me in my office and explained what had happened. She said Leo had just called her and gave her the good news. My mouth fell open at the prognosis, and I was so happy and relieved for Miles and Leo.

"Listen, I hope I'm not being too forward," Natalie said, "but Leo told me about the history between the three of you. I know he wants to talk to you himself, but I wanted to say I'm glad you and Miles found each other again. He's the happiest I've seen him since I've known him. And he's a good guy. He deserves to be happy."

I smiled at her. "Thanks for that. I'm glad Leo found you. You seem to have cracked the code with him."

She laughed. "It took some work, but I found the sweet guy in there, and he's a keeper now."

"Good, I'm happy for you both," I told her, meaning it. Even though he was a complete asshole to me, he and Natalie seemed happy. I still wasn't sure what the commotion was all about between him and Miles at the pool, but since Natalie wasn't the least bit upset by it anymore, I guessed it all got smoothed over. As far as I could tell, the Townsend family was long overdue for some smoother roads.

Once Natalie left, Julian appeared, wanting to know what the fiancée had to say.

"Sorry to disappoint you, but it wasn't a real housewives reunion if that's what you're hoping for."

"I would never want that for you! That would stress you out too much. I know you probably view it differently because of my flair for the dramatic, but I always want what's best for you and what makes you happy."

I smiled at him. "I know, and I love you for that."

"Good, remember that when I tell you—you need to quit being so hard on yourself, Paige. It's all going to work out."

I sighed and reminded him it was easy for him to say because he always had a soft place to land. And then I admitted to both him and myself, "Sometimes I wish you never brought Miles and his family here. It's been nothing but chaos," I paused, searching for the right words and admitting to myself for the first time out loud, "but honestly, I'm so grateful to you. I mean, what are the odds you would bring this guy I've been pining over for years back to me? And I feel terrible because I've been pushing him away, and I'm sure he has to be terribly confused. But I've made my whole life about work, and I've been so terrified that I would turn back into the pushover I was when I was younger that I've been running from Miles. But I'm realizing that when it's the right person, they bring out the best in you. As much as I love Miles, I could never be a doormat for him, and I don't think he would ever let me."

Julian's eyes widened, and his eyebrows shot up. "Did you just say ..."

I bit my lip before letting loose a smile. "Yeah, I did. I love him. I never knew I could love someone this way, and that makes me believe we have a chance. Maybe it's not some disaster waiting to happen."

He rolled his eyes. "You're such a poet, Paige. Word of advice, when you're telling all of this to Miles, maybe leave out the part about disaster waiting to happen."

I laughed, then straightened from my chair. "Noted."

Julian clapped hands together with a wide grin. "Well, no time like the present. Why don't you go see if your boy toy has come back and then profess your love, followed by some rowdy, raunchy sex?"

I rolled my eyes at Julian. "That really is all you think about, isn't it?"

He laughed wickedly. "Of course, when you're built like Danny and myself, it's hard to think of much else," he said with a wink.

"Eww, and double eww. But you're right—I should go find Miles."

And with that, I left my office, fighting and losing the battle to keep the stupid grin off my face as I floated to the elevator. But my mood briefly dampened when Irene intercepted me to inform me of a minor problem. Which was followed by another small fire to put out and then another. It wasn't until an hour and a half later I could finally make my way to the second floor and knock on Miles's door. Only when I got there, the door was slightly ajar.

"Miles?" I said, knocking on the door and popping my head in. "Miles?" I called again, seeing that nobody was there.

The room was abandoned. No luggage, nothing except for a bright white folded piece of paper leaning against the pillow.

I looked closer and saw it had my name scrawled on it.

With trembling hands, I picked it up and opened the paper, and a picture of me fell to the floor. It was a picture of when I was much younger—a picture I'd given to Leo when we were dating.

My eyes devoured the words on the page:

Paige,

This picture has helped me through so many difficult times. I swiped it from Leo's dresser the night after we made love for the first time, and I have carried it against my heart every day since. Just as I will carry you inside my heart for the rest of my life ... I don't need this picture anymore because it's a reminder of what I lost. I regret that my family and I have caused you so much trouble and ruined your grand opening, putting the resort at risk. All I've ever wanted was to help and be your biggest supporter, not get in your way.

You were meant to fly high, Paige Russell, higher than me, and the last thing you need is somebody weighing you down. Thank you for these last few precious days together. The sweet memories will last a lifetime, and I'm grateful I got to experience them with you, even if only for a little while.

And on those days when nothing is going right, please take comfort knowing I love you, and I will always love you.

Love, Miles

My head jerked up from reading the paper, but I saw nothing before me. My vision was too blurry, the tears streaming down my face.

I was too late.

He was gone.

I let out a quiet sob and jumped when I heard a knock. I turned around, hoping to God it was Miles, only to see Leo standing in the doorway.

"Paige? What happened?"

I didn't know what to do. I didn't understand what was happening, so I handed him the letter. He read it, his expression turning sour. "That idiot," he said with a sigh. Then he looked up at me, sympathy in his eyes. "Listen, Paige, I just had a conversation with him about how he was going to come after you, whisk you away, and make you his forever. So there's gotta be something else going on here. I'll talk to him, and we'll straighten this out, okay?" he promised.

I was shaking my head, looking at him, confused. "Why would you do that? You saw the letter. He said goodbye."

Leo huffed. "He's being dramatic. And I would do that because I care for you, and I love my big brother."

I looked at him dubiously.

"I totally understand why you would doubt me, considering how I treated you in the past, but that's why I've been looking for you. I know I've been acting strange this week, but I've been trying to work up the nerve to apologize."

"Apologize?"

"Yes. It's long overdue," he said. "I hate the guy I was when we were together, and unfortunately, I was that guy much longer than I care to admit. When I met Natalie, I turned over a new leaf, and I realized how many people I'd hurt before she came into my life. The thought of anybody treating Natalie the way I treated so many women kills me. And I wish I could go back and tell my younger self to get his head out of his ass. You didn't deserve to be treated so poorly, and I'm sorry for that."

What the hell was happening? It was like whiplash between the letter from Miles and Leo apologizing.

"I totally get it if you don't forgive me. I know you have a lot on your plate at the moment, but I wanted you to know I was a fool back then, and I'm trying to clean up my act. I'm glad you found somebody who truly appreciates you, and believe me when I say that is my brother. Something must have spooked him, but he's a smart guy. I'll get him to come around."

I looked at him glumly. "I'm not so sure ... I kept pushing him away because I was gun-shy. I was terrified he would hurt me."

Leo nodded in understanding. "I hate the hand I've had in that, but I'm going to fix it, Paige."

With that, he rushed out the door, leaving me standing in Miles' room with the letter in one hand and the picture in the other.

Suddenly, Mia burst through the door sans wig and German accent. "I just ran into Leo. He told me what happened and that you needed me."

I looked at her, stunned, and she smiled. "It turns out he knew it was me the whole time, but hey, at least he didn't out me," she said, shrugging her shoulders. Then she was pulling me into her arms as I sobbed onto her shoulder. She rubbed my back as she kept telling me in soothing tones, "It's going to be okay, Paige. It's all going to work out, don't worry."

I appreciated her words, and it took me back to the last time my heart had been broken, although it paled in comparison. Back then, I had enough hope in me to believe her words. But now they fell flat. Nothing would ever be the same again, not after having known the joys and pleasures of having Miles in my life.

Nothing could hold a candle to the few days I'd spent with my fantasy man. Only now that was over, and it was time to come back to reality—and my reality didn't have Miles in it.

MILES

"Dude, you are an idiot," Leo admonished sternly to me over FaceTime.

I opened my mouth to speak, but then Natalie appeared. "I think what he meant to say was there's been some miscommunication. That seems to run rampant in this family," she added with a frown.

"What are you talking about? Is Dad okay?"

"Of course he is, but where the hell are you?"

"I went home. When I spoke to Mom, she said it was fine because they were only allowing her to visit for now. I figured I could help get the house ready for Dad when he gets home," I explained, fighting the weight on my chest. It was more than that, of course, so much more, but I wasn't about to admit that to my brother or his fiancée.

"Bullshit," Leo said. "You're running away. I saw the letter you gave Paige."

"She showed you that?"

"Yeah. She didn't know what to do with herself. When I found her, she couldn't speak because she was crying so hard, so she just handed it to me. Nice job, bro. I felt bad for breaking her heart, but it's nothing compared to what you just did."

Natalie gave her fiancé a stern look, and Leo toned it down. "Right, sorry. I've been informed I can be a little too harsh sometimes. But seriously, dude, what the fuck? You're supposed to be the smarter of the two of us."

I shook my head. "Not that it's any of your business, but I overheard Paige saying she wished we'd never shown up at her resort. The last thing I want to do is to be somewhere I'm not wanted."

Natalie grabbed the phone from Leo. "Miles, listen to me. I know we don't know each other well, and I don't know Paige at all, but I did speak with her earlier today, and she admitted to me she's in love with you. A woman doesn't share her feelings like that if she's not hoping for something to come of it. Did you ask her about what you overheard?"

I shook my head. "No," I admitted. "Her office door was open. I overheard her talking to Julian about how we had brought all this chaos to the resort."

"Well, to be fair, we did," Leo said.

"Yes," Natalie added. "And as a former attorney, you should appreciate that context matters. You hear one snippet of a conversation, and you don't give her a chance to clarify? That's hardly fair, Miles."

I sighed, shaking my head.

"She's right, man," Leo added.

"Did she really say she loved me?"

Both Natalie and Leo nodded. "She said it to Nat, she said it to me, and I could hear her crying to Julian and Mia not long after I talked to her."

Everything in me seized up out of terror, yet a hopeful bloom pushed through the fear. She loved me? It wasn't one-sided?

"I fucked up," I breathed out.

Leo and Natalie glanced at each other. "Sure did," Leo confirmed.

"That's real helpful, babe," Natalie said, then turned toward the camera. "It's not too late, Miles. You need to talk to her. And all things considered, a grand gesture might not be a bad idea."

"A grand gesture?"

"Yep," Leo said. "And I don't think flowers and chocolates will get it done. If I remember Paige correctly, she tends to overthink, so you need to do something huge to leave no doubt in her mind that you're serious about loving her."

I looked at the two of them, agitated and panicky, and that was when I heard my future sister-in-law's voice reach out to me, "Miles, take a breath. We got a family think tank going on here. We will figure this out. Don't worry."

I could see why Leo fell for her. She was kind and compassionate and took charge when necessary, which was perfect for Leo. A phone call that started off making me feel both devastated and euphoric had turned into an all-out planning session for declaring my love to Paige Russell.

The Townsend family may have brought chaos to her resort, but in no time, we would be raining love all over it instead.

PAIGE

Twenty-four hours later ...

I didn't know what to do. I picked up the phone and almost called or texted Miles a million times, but before Leo had left with Natalie, he'd urged me to let him handle it, and for the first time in my life, I would trust Leo.

He and Natalie were certain about their mission, and I hated they felt like they needed to take it on. There was so much going on with Mr. Townsend, but Natalie assured me there wasn't a lot to do other than be supportive as Mr. Townsend recuperated in the hospital with Lucy by his side. She had arranged for everything to be set up for Mr. and Mrs. Townsend so when they returned home, Walter would be comfortable. They were hell-bent on playing Cupid for Miles and me. I wasn't sure what to think, but Julian, Mia, and Danny reassured me to wait and "see what happened."

I might not have had a clue what I was doing in my love life, but I knew how to run a business, so I threw myself into work for the next twenty-four hours. For the first time since I had been in charge of Ambrose Vineyards, it wasn't enough to distract me. The guests were happy with the extra amenities, and I was determined to make something good come out of the mess because, evidently, the place would be my only love now that I had chased away Miles.

My resolve vanished once night fell, and I roamed the empty hall-ways. The guests had scattered to their respective rooms or had gone out for the evening, and I walked through the resort until I came out the exit that led me to the row of vines where Miles and I had made love under the stars.

The tears I'd been holding back all day streamed freely. How had I gotten it so wrong? When I was offered Ambrose Vineyards, I knew it was a once-in-a-lifetime opportunity, and I'd understood that some-times you had to jump even if you were not quite ready for it. That had been my philosophy with every venture Julian and I had embarked upon since taking over the vineyard, but somehow, that hadn't trans-lated to my personal life.

With my personal life, I shrunk away in fear in the face of oppor-tunity. I wasn't prepared for Miles and the love he offered. Something in me was absolutely certain I would screw it up somehow.

My eyes wandered toward the darkened vines, and the realization hit—it wasn't just relationships I feared. I'd built Miles up so large in my mind that actually embarking on a real-life adventure with him terrified me. It scared me to think I wouldn't live up to the expecta-tions he'd built up in his head, and it was easy to blame poor timing when I pushed him away. It hurt when I wasn't enough for Leo, but I knew I wouldn't survive not being enough for Miles.

Then I remembered the words in his note: "I will always love you ..."

It had been a little over a day since he'd left, and it had felt like an eternity. It made those eight years I'd gone without him seem like seconds, and I didn't know how I would carry on. Things were different now. Miles changed my life. Again.

Suddenly, the allure and shine of our brand new resort wasn't so thrilling anymore, not if I couldn't share it with Miles.

I plopped down on the ground, pulling my knees to my chest, and I let myself weep. When I felt all cried out, I stumbled back to my house and fell into an exhausted heap on my couch. When I closed my eyes, I'd been certain I would never fall asleep, but I lapsed into an exhausted stupor and dreamed of Miles—reaching for him but never quite being able to make contact.

The next day, I cleaned myself up and got ready for another day of work. I walked around my house, reciting all the things that needed to be taken care of. Suddenly, my never-ending to-do list was a comfort. Hopefully, I would be able to think about something other than Miles for longer than five seconds.

My hopes were dashed when I entered the kitchen. The kitchen staff was behaving oddly. I met Chef Martha's gaze, but she looked at me perturbed. "Somebody has been in my kitchen," she said, gesturing to the cutting board in front of her. "Did you let your beau in here again, Paige? He's the only one who mangles peppers like this," she said sternly, pointing at a mangled pepper.

My brow furrowed. "Do you think somebody broke into the kitchen to mess with your peppers?" I asked, but then Martha shoved the chopping board over to me, and I saw the peppers weren't mangled. They were making the shape of a ... "Is that a heart?" I asked, giggling.

Chef Martha stiffened and looked at me primly. "This is no laughing matter, Paige. The least you could do is inspect the premises to make sure nothing else has been tampered with."

I shook my head. "Right, I'll get right on that."

I'd taken only a few steps out of the kitchen before Julian rushed toward me. "Am I glad to see you! That stupid leaky pipe is at it again!"

I muttered a curse under my breath and rushed to the lounge. "I'm hoping it's not too bad. It's Friday. We'll have a hell of a time getting somebody here today," I said.

What I found, however, made me start in confusion. There was no water leak, but a handwritten "Miles loves Paige" in chalk on the concrete.

My heart did a funny little flip, and I looked back at Julian, who was smiling at me. "What's going on here?"

He shrugged. "I'm not sure I know what you mean, but Danny reported an issue in the vineyard, somewhere in the third row ..."

I felt heat creep up my cheeks. That was the exact location where Miles and I had rediscovered one another.

Part of me wanted to stop and grill him, but my feet had other ideas as I rushed toward the vineyard. Once I got to the location, I stopped cold when I saw what was waiting for me. It was another heart. Except this time, it was a grapevine artfully sculpted and laid out on the exact same spot I'd been laid out by Miles.

I turned behind me to see Julian, Mia, and Danny standing there, smiling.

"What on earth is going on?"

"That's something you will have to figure out for yourself ... although you may want to look up in four, three, two, one," Mia counted down. And that was when I heard it, the buzzing of a small plane. I looked up into the sky, shielding my eyes, and saw the small plane soaring over the field with a banner trailing behind it that read, "I love you, Paige, forever and always."

My hands dropped to my side, and I turned back to my friends. "I told you it would all work out," Julian said.

"I can't believe this," I breathed.

"Well, believe it because it's happening, and you deserve it all, my dear friend," Mia said, hugging me.

I hugged her back and looked up, watching the plane go by again, waving to it frantically.

"I can't believe you all were a part of this," I said.

"We're your family. Of course, we'd be a part of this. In fact, we'll probably be a much too invasive part of your relationship, too," Mia added, winking at me.

The plane went by once more and then disappeared, and a few minutes later, my friends backed away. "We're going to go ... do some stuff," Danny said.

"That's right, but you should stay right there," Mia added.

I smiled as I watched them go away. They were giggling like schoolchildren as they headed back to the resort.

I waited for a few moments, twisting my hands together. And then he was there. My dream man materialized out of thin air. "Miles," I breathed.

He said my name, and then I launched myself into his arms before I could stop myself.

Holding me to him, he twirled me around in a circle.

When he set me down, he was already talking. "I'm so sorry I just took off. I overheard you talking to Julian about how you wished we hadn't shown up, and I panicked. I hate we caused so much trouble for you, and I didn't want to be in your way."

"What? That's ridiculous. I was venting about how chaotic everything has been, but the next time you eavesdrop, listen to the whole thing," I said, swatting at him playfully. "Because then you would've heard me tell him how grateful I was that he sprung you on me. How grateful I was for all the chaos because it meant I got you, and we had a second chance."

His grin widened. "You have no idea how good it is to hear say that. My soon-to-be sister-in-law pointed out I should've talked to you first before running away."

"Well, yes, she's right. And Miles, the next time you're concerned about something, please promise me you'll talk to me."

"I promise," he said, stepping closer to me, his eyes alternating between my eyes and my mouth, "just like I promise to love you forever."

I looked at him for a long moment, "I'm going to take a leap of faith and believe you mean that ... because I love you, too."

He let out a whoop of joy, gathered me up in his arms, and kissed me. And that kiss was the official beginning of our forever ... Complete with applause and cheers from my friends a few yards away.

Epilogue

One year later …

The last year of my life was the busiest yet.

After Miles and I reunited, it was a whirlwind of finalizing the official grand opening of the resort and moving him to Sonoma.

Maybe we should've taken it slow, but I moved him right into my house. After all our years apart, it seemed only appropriate to make up for lost time. I wanted him there with me at Ambrose Vineyards, the place where we were building a life together.

Business at the resort was booming. Much to my surprise, Misty, the travel blogger who had visited during that fateful week with Miles' family, gave the resort a glowing review. It took a surprise turn when she dedicated several passages to the resort hostess who'd been quick in doing first aid and saved a guest's life. She'd waxed euphoric about how the proprietors of Ambrose Vineyards went above and beyond to make it feel like a fun family experience. Between her glowing review and Miles's father telling all his golf buddies, high-rolling clients, and colleagues about the resort, we had a six-month waiting list.

Miles kept more than busy flying back and forth from Los Angeles to bring guests to our vineyard and resort. It was so lovely to share our little piece of paradise with guests, and Julian and I were constantly coming up with new ideas to make it better.

The next event we were holding at the resort was really special to us—Leo and Natalie's wedding was only a week away. Lucy had taken near-permanent residence in her own special room at the resort as she helped to coordinate all the vendors for the wedding.

So, with all the hubbub going on inside the resort between the guests and the wedding planning, I was relieved when Miles had urged me to meet him one evening at "our spot" in the vineyard. It was definitely time for a moment away from all the chaos, even though I loved it. We snuck away like two children sneaking away from their families, giggling in the night. But our spot didn't look like it usually did.

There was a picnic blanket laid out and candles in the shape of a heart. I turned to Miles to ask, "What is this?" But the words died on my lips when I saw he was down on one knee and had a small velvet box in his hands.

"Miles?"

"Paige, I waited for you for so long, and it was worth every second. Once you told me you loved me, I didn't think I could want anything more, but there is one more thing ... I want you to be my wife. Paige Elizabeth Russell, will you marry me?"

He barely got the last part out before I screamed out. "Yes!" I pulled him up and then pulled him into my arms. "Of course, I'll be your wife. I want nothing more than for you to be my husband," I said, wrapping my arms around his neck and pulling him down for a deep, lingering kiss.

I meant to pull back and tell him how happy he made me. I meant to vow I would love him forever, but none of that came out in words. Instead, we were falling to the earth next to the candles, frantically removing one another's clothes, and I felt like I could breathe again when he pushed inside me and began moving.

Maybe those words didn't need to be said by our mouths when our bodies were doing the talking. He stared down into my eyes as he moved deliberately inside me. I loved how he could convey his fire and desire with just one look.

The man loved me. I knew it and never had to question it.

After exploding intensely against one another, we clung to one another, whispering soft words of love.

"It really was a miracle," I said, referring to how we had found one another again.

He pulled back, looking into my eyes and smiling. "Was it? Or was it just meant to be?"

THE END

Dear Reader,

Thank you from the bottom of my heart for taking the time to dive into this beautiful world with me. I hope it has touched your heart, brought you joy, and provided a little bit of that delicious thrill that only a good steamy scene can deliver.

Creating Paige and Miles, their passionate encounters, and emotional depth has been a labor of love. I hope you found their love story as intoxicating as I did.

It's because of you, my incredible readers, that this book came to life, and for that, I am forever grateful.

If you enjoyed your time in Sonoma, I would be so thankful if you would take a few moments to leave a review on Amazon.

Your feedback not only helps other readers find and fall in love with this story, but it also fuels my creativity and keeps me excited to bring you more. It doesn't have to be lengthy—a few words are enough to make a significant impact!

Scan the code below to leave your review.

Thank you again for being the most wonderful part of my career as an author. Here's to more thrilling rides and romantic nights!

With all my love and a million thanks,
Ana

Thank you for reading **Second Chance with My Ex's Brother**.

If you liked this book, then you will love **Rebuilding Forever**!

Why you'll love it...

* Single mom

* HS sweethearts
* Second chance
* Protective hero
* Secret identity

In a town too small for secrets, he's back.
My heart's biggest mistake. And now my greatest temptation.

Liam was my first love, the one who promised me forever—then left.
Now he's back, fixing up his late father's house.

I know once he finishes what he came here to do, he'll disappear again.
But I can't resist him—the fire in his eyes drawing me straight into his
arms.

Despite a messy divorce, I'm keeping it together for my little girl.
Only neither one of us can afford another heartbreak.

When a storm destroys my kitchen—and my livelihood—Liam takes
us in.
It feels like we finally got the family we always wanted, until his secret
threatens to destroy everything.

**Can we rebuild what we had, or has he broken my trust for the
last time?**

Scan HERE to get your copy!

SNEAK PEEK
REBUILDING
FOREVER

Three months ago...

I worked my way carefully over the patches of ice, silently willing warmer temperatures to come through Palmer. The snow was a treat during the holidays, but when it lingered into March, I got sick of its "magic".

Plus, the ice and the overcast sky took on an even more ominous feel today as I worked my way over the frozen patches of grass to the fresh grave in Union Cemetery.

It felt like the whole town was at the funeral and even though I might have been able to go undetected amongst all the people, I stayed away.

Patrick Murphy, a pillar of our small community, had unexpectedly passed away the week before. One of his poker buddies got worried when he didn't show up for his weekly game and found him at home in the recliner.

The town doctor said it was a heart attack. I hated the idea of him dying alone at home, but I was grateful it was quick. The last thing I wanted to imagine was Patrick suffering.

Standing before his grave, I said a quick prayer and placed a rose on top of the new tombstone. Liam had done an excellent job—it was simple but tasteful, something Patrick would have liked.

Chills went up my spine knowing that Liam was somewhere in Palmer. Until today, I had the comfort of knowing he wouldn't be coming back here. When he left thirteen years ago, that was it. No visits, no phone calls... just gone. Patrick would fly to Austin a few times a year to see him, but Liam had meant it when he said he was never coming back to Palmer.

I tried not to focus on that. The heartache he caused still hurt, even after all these years. I feel like I've lived an entire lifetime since then. I've been married and divorced and am now raising the most amazing daughter I could ever hope for. Today isn't about our teenaged love gone awry. It's about the man finally resting in peace.

Patrick and I had stayed close over the years. It had been difficult at first—I couldn't see him without thinking about Liam. But he was all by himself. Liam's mom died when he was a baby and it had always been just the two of them. Once Liam left, I felt bad knowing Patrick was wandering around that big old house by himself.

I made a habit of saying hi when I saw him around town and eventually, when I started my baking business, I always made a little extra for Patrick. He was my unbiased taste tester. He would tell me when something worked, or it tasted awful.

We had only gotten closer since my ex-husband left. I think he felt bad Abigail didn't have a dad. Although it's not like I ever had one, so I guess I kept up the family tradition on that one.

Patrick stepped in as a grandfatherly figure to Abigail. He even dressed up as Santa the last few years and tiptoed around the front porch so Abigail would catch him with his large velvet sack slung over his shoulder.

I would forever be grateful to Patrick for that. For a time when I was younger, I thought Patrick would become my family, but all that changed when Liam ran off. When I came back to Palmer after my divorce, Patrick was one of the first people to welcome me home with open arms.

I wish I could say it was the same with everyone else in town, but he was one of only a few who stepped in to help. We had an unspoken agreement that discussing Liam was off the table. There was no question about who had ended things. When Liam decided to leave, I'd begged him like a fool to stay. It's a memory that still makes my face burn with embarrassment.

But Liam evidently meant what he said about needing to get out of Palmer, because once he left, he was gone for good. When Liam eventually settled in Austin and Patrick would go to visit, he'd asked me to check on his house to make sure nothing was amiss. When he returned, he would say his trip was "good" sparing the details of how Liam was. I appreciated the gesture.

Maybe it was silly of me. It had been thirteen years since Liam left, and we were kids. But there are moments when it doesn't feel like all those years have passed. When it didn't feel like I'd survived a marriage and a divorce and had already gotten a child out of diapers. There were moments when I closed my eyes and I could still feel the thrill of excitement that raced through me at the touch of Liam's fingertips skating down my skin.

That touch had felt like home to me then, and in my more vulnerable moments, I could admit to myself it still did. That was back when I believed that every touch was a promise for the future, which made all of his little touches even more exciting. It didn't matter that we would struggle. It didn't matter that we would never be rich. I didn't care about any of it, even though my mother had voiced plenty of concern over it. No, it thrilled me to endure whatever struggle was necessary if it meant Liam and I would be together.

I shook my head free of my thoughts. Now was not the time to reminisce about an old love, especially one who had betrayed me.

I focused my attention on the grave marker before me and made a vow to Mr. Murphy: "I'll make you proud, Patrick. What are we going to do without you? I would've brought Abigail, but I didn't think she was ready. Thank you for supporting me when others didn't and for stepping in when you didn't have to. I will always love you for that."

I looked down at the bloom in my hand, a single white rose. I don't know why, but it seemed like the most fitting one for Patrick.

Swallowing around the lump in my throat, I placed the rose on top of his marker and stepped back, swiping at the tears streaming down my cheeks.

I started to turn away when something stopped me. I hadn't done it before because I thought it might be silly, but I decided to go for it. I dug into my bag and produced a little cardboard bakery box.

Inside was Patrick's favorite flavor of cupcake: chocolate brownie, with caramel ganache and extra sprinkles.

I sat it down next to the rose. "Here you go, one for the road."

That's when my emotions overwhelmed me and I hurried away, barely seeing through the blur of tears.

I was in such a rush, I almost slipped on a patch of ice, but I caught myself. It was in that moment I stopped to look around. I was certain I had been alone in my conversation with Patrick, but I couldn't shake the feeling that someone was watching me.

I looked around the abandoned cemetery. Nobody in sight, just me and the sound of my ragged breath.

I looked back at Patrick's grave. Maybe it was him, I thought to myself. Maybe that was his little tap on the shoulder, telling me to be careful as I crossed those icy patches. It seemed like something he would do.

But as I got back to my car and made my way home, I couldn't shake the feeling of being watched. It had to be my imagination getting the better of me.

For the first time in years, Liam Murphy was nearby. That I could feel his presence so keenly everywhere just reminded me how awful the heartbreak had been. It cut deeper than signing the divorce papers from my ex-husband.

But today was about laying Patrick to rest, not reminiscing about Liam, I reminded myself.

It still didn't seem real that he was gone. Just a week ago, Patrick stopped by the house to tell me the latest recipe I dropped off was going "to be the one." Of course, he always said that. He would try out my recipes with a relish, and then swear up and down it would be the one to catapult me to business stardom.

In fact, he was the one who encouraged me to think about getting a storefront. My mother was against the idea, telling me the upkeep would be too much for me as a single mom. But Patrick disagreed. He promised as soon as I got enough money together to open my store, he'd help me with whatever repairs needed to be done or appliances installed.

The cupcake had been my daughter's idea, and I made it with a flavor combination he had suggested the day before he died.

I should've checked in on him more, I thought to myself. I should've made sure he was taking his meds. He had a heart defect his whole life. The local doctor said he had a pretty good run, considering he'd been carrying that around all these years. But that gave me little solace. It seemed unfair that somebody so good and kind didn't have more time on this earth to enjoy the town he loved so much.

Patrick had been the town's local carpenter for years. It never made him rich, and sometimes he struggled to put food on the table, but he was easily the happiest person I knew. He'd grown up in these mountains. He knew how to hunt, exactly what plants to stay away from, and what could sustain an empty belly for a while.

Liam's mom had died during childbirth. It had always been just him and his dad. While I knew Patrick missed his wife Molly more than anything, he never got down about it.

He told me he didn't have time to be depressed about it because he had a baby to take care of. He said he got a blanket and wrapped it around him the way he'd seen his mother do with his many brothers and sisters. Then he fashioned a little baby Bjorn, strapped it to his chest, and carried on with work.

"I'm sure it was an OSHA violation, but I never let him too close to anything that might hurt him. And that boy could swing a hammer properly before he could walk," he always reported proudly. And he'd been right about that. Liam was just as handy as his father and seemed destined to follow in his footsteps.

But that had been a sticking point for my mother.

I hated her for it back then, but now, as a single mother, I can understand her concern. My dad left when I was young, leaving my mom to figure it all out, and we struggled. She resented him for that and always told me I needed to make sure I found somebody who would take care of me.

She didn't see that in Liam Murphy. She didn't see people who foraged and scrounged as innovative and self-sufficient. They were poor and the last thing she would ever allow was sending her daughter off with some poor boy.

I still have some anger in my heart over that. Because for all of her advice to find a husband who could "take care of me", here I was a single mom, just like she'd been, struggling to make ends meet. Mama figured I'd hit the jackpot when I married a law student. It never occurred to her that even a rich husband can leave his wife and child at a moment's notice—with nothing.

For all of her fussing about Liam, it sounds like he did pretty well for himself in Texas. I don't think he was rolling in lawyer money, but he had a roof over his head, and was doing just fine. Not that it mattered. I wasn't interested in any man's money. I was only interested in caring for my family and making sure my daughter and I were okay.

I hadn't realized it at the time, but Patrick's presence provided stability for Abigail and myself that was gone now. I wondered if I could pull this off without his gentle, guiding hand.

A few days after the funeral, Abigail and I were bustling out the door, running late as usual to get her to school, when Abigail squawked out my name that made me jump out of my skin.

My heart started pounding, as most parents do when their kids make that sound. "Abigail, what's wrong, baby?"

Abigail was pointing to our porch railing. There, right next to the finial, was one of my white bakery boxes. It was the same one I'd left on Patrick's grave marker. Abigail had drawn a picture on the outside and wrote a message for him.

We looked at each other with wide eyes, and then I shook my head and hurried to the railing.

Gingerly, I picked up the box. It was lightweight now—the heft of the cupcake was gone.

I threw a reassuring smile over my shoulder at Abigail and opened the box. Indeed, the cupcake was gone, a couple of chocolate stains on the edges of the box remained, and a note folded neatly in its place.

I plucked the piece of paper out and unfolded it. It was shaking in my hands. It read in a familiar handwriting, "Thank you for the cupcake. That flavor is a winner, don't forget it. I love you always."

"Mommy? You're crying. What does it say?"

I quickly swept away the tears and assured Abigail they were happy tears. I read the note to her, and she looked up at me, confused as I rushed to explain, "I think Patrick wanted you to know he loves you and he's watching over you."

I wasn't sure if that was the right thing to say. I often felt that way as a parent, but I was rewarded with Abigail's serene smile and her steps seemed to pick up a little as we walked to the car. She had a million questions about where Patrick was and what he must be doing, and I tried to answer them as best as I could. But when I kissed her goodbye for the day, my mind immediately went back to the familiar handwriting on the note.

I'd seen that handwriting on a hundred notes, all proclaiming their love.

I shook my head. I doubt Patrick kept it a secret he was close to me and my daughter. And I'm sure from the drawings on the sides of the box, Liam understood somebody would be missing his dad almost as much as he did.

It was such a Liam move. His dad would have been proud—reaching out to console a little girl who he didn't know.

And even though I knew that was all it could be, I couldn't help but feel haunted by the words "love you always."

Once upon a time, Liam had promised me that very thing, but it wasn't enough to make him stay. He shot out of this town like a cannon the first opportunity he got, leaving me in the dust.

I bolstered my resolve with that reminder. He'd made a kind gesture to a little girl, and it was sweet, but it didn't change that he had run away from me.

Scan HERE to get your copy!

Keep In Touch

Want to stay up to date on all things Ana Rhodes? Join her newsletter! Get exclusive access to bonus content, cover reveals, excerpts, news and giveaways.

SCAN to subscribe!

Let's be friends on social media:
https://www.instagram.com/anarhodesauthor/
https://www.facebook.com/anarhodeswrites
https://www.goodreads.com/author/show/42608432.Ana_Rhodes